SPLIT DECISION

You are so there.

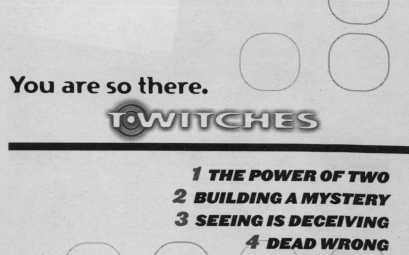

T·WITCHES

T*WITCHES

H.B. GILMOUR
& RANDI REISFELD

SCHOLASTIC INC.
NEW YORK   TORONTO   LONDON   AUCKLAND   SYDNEY
MEXICO CITY   NEW DELHI   HONG KONG   BUENOS AIRES

ISBN 0-439-49230-0

12 11 10 9 8 7 6 5 4 3 2 1   3 4 5 6 7 8/0

PRINTED IN THE U.S.A.   40
FIRST PRINTING, SEPTEMBER 2003

 **SPLIT DECISION**

CHAPTER ONE
FIRESTARTER

Against a backdrop of a royal-blue sky, fireworks lit up the night. Bursting bouquets of orange, fiery red, blinding silver, and glittering gold rained down on the awestruck crowd. It was the Fourth of July in Marble Bay, Massachusetts, and nearly the entire town had turned out for the show. Neighbors for the night, they formed a united chorus of ooohhs and aaahhhs as crackling geysers of color erupted over the water. This night on the beach, the spirit of friendship was infectious.

And Camryn Barnes had never felt so alone.

Cue the cliché, the striking auburn-haired teen thought. You *can* feel loneliest in a crowd. Even when the crowd is your own. Cam sat on a blanket, scrunched between her five best friends. Her intense charcoal-gray eyes were trained on the awesome fireworks, but her thoughts had elsewhere to be. They dragged her to places she didn't want to go.

So he was gone. So what? Not that far, and not forever. Jason Weissman had left early for college. It wasn't as if they'd ever been an official couple. This hollow feeling, then, couldn't be about Jason.

A loud boom shook the sky. Interlocking rings of fireworks exploded. Shimmering blue sparklers lit the sky, followed by blasts of blinding white, then red rockets flashed dazzlingly. United in patriotism and excitement, the crowd roared its approval.

Where do fireworks go once they've landed? Cam wondered idly. They just scatter and disappear, she supposed.

Like her friends were about to do. Fireworks on the Fourth kicked off the official start of summer — this one marked the time between sophomore and junior years of high school for Cam's crew. It also marked their first summer apart.

Amanda was going up north to work at a sleepaway camp. Beth was headed down to Florida, where her recently divorced dad had moved. Sukari was zooming east, where an archaeological dig in Europe awaited. Brianna and Kristen, west to some pricey tennis camp, courtesy of Bree's Hollywood producer dad. (The man who'd rather throw money Bree's way than give her the time of his day.)

Cam wasn't going anywhere.

This year's summer vacation had been scuttled, a fallout of belt-tightening, her adoptive dad, Dave, explained. Her mom, Emily, made it even clearer. With a third college-bound child to care for — that would be Alex, who'd showed up on their doorstep a year ago — instead of just two (Cam and her brother, Dylan), blowing big bucks for a summer jaunt seemed irresponsible. So Cam was slated for a stay-at-home. Was the empty feeling in the pit of her stomach all about jealousy?

Nuh-uh. Cam had never been about the "poor little me" thing. Yet here she was down in Dumpsville, on the off-ramp to Pity City.

One good thing, none of her friends saw through her.

They never had.

Cam had always been the sunny-side-up girl on the outside, even though on the inside she'd thought something was wrong with her; all her life she'd known she was different.

She'd been right. When Alex — the identical twin she'd never met and hadn't known about — came into her life at age fourteen, everything all of a sudden made sense. A stranger from the other side of the country, a girl who'd experienced identical weirdness. *That* was what had been missing. Reunited, both had felt, if not exactly normal, at least whole, for the first time ever.

"Snacks! We need munchies!" Curly-haired Beth busted in on Cam's reverie.

"Agua," Kristen piped up. "We need drinks. We are parched."

Sukari perched on one knee and peered around. "Check it out. The snack cart is as far from here as it could be. I calculate five hundred yards, and that doesn't take into account the X factor —"

"The X factor? You actually just said that?" Brianna marveled. "Is that what they mean by 'of course you'll use algebra in real life'?"

Sukari ignored her. "The X factor is the maze of people separating us from our munchies. It's gonna take guts and determination to negotiate this obstacle course."

"I'll go," Cam quickly volunteered.

Brianna approved. "Excellent. Gutsy Camryn will fetch."

When the girls had placed their orders, Beth noted, "That's a lot to tote back. I'll come with."

Cam got to her feet and pretend-deepened her voice. "I am your leader. I accept my responsibility as the bringer of all things sweet and caloric."

"Done deal," Brianna cut to the chase. "So it'll be five Pepsis and —"

"They're out of Pepsi," Cam said absentmindedly, eyeing the food cart.

"Then get — wait, rewind," Bree challenged. "You can't see that from here."

Actually, Cam could. She could see not only the lack of Pepsi but everything on the cart, down to the change — two quarters and a dime — being given to a customer. Her telescopic, zoom-lens eyesight was a gift her friends could never know about. Thinking quickly, she said, "I just heard someone say they only had iced tea and those red-white-and-blue slushies left."

Bree rolled her emerald eyes. "Whatever. So make it four slushies and —"

"One diet iced tea," Cam anticipated Bree's request. The girl least likely to need fewer calories continued to monitor them, her eating disorder under control, but not cured.

Nor was this unsettled ache. Cam was relieved to have an excuse to leave her friends for a bit. Threading her way through the crowd, she flipped through possibilities. Was it her friends leaving or was it Jason?

He's here! Pinch me. He came back. For me!

Cam stopped short. For one microsecond, she'd imagined those excited thoughts were hers. But no. They were owned and operated exclusively by her twin sister, Alex.

Alexandra Fielding. The name called up images of a decked-out debutante gracefully descending a staircase for her coming-out gala.

That would not be *this* Alexandra Fielding. Like Cam's twin might ever be seen out of uniform — faded, torn jeans, frayed camo top, and scrungy mocs.

Her sister lived by her own set of standards and practices. Take tonight. Als had been invited to watch the fireworks with the gang but hadn't even made a "just to be social" cameo.

Okay, so this time she had a good reason. Cam's bio-twin was enveloped and enraptured by a boy she'd known only briefly before he bolted for Paris, a boy named Cade, who'd come back. For the summer, at least. For Alex, at most.

Cam hadn't meant to tap into Alex's joy, but she couldn't help herself. Correction: Didn't help herself.

She and Alex could read each other's minds. Really, though, like regular identical twins, who can sometimes sense things. Alex and Cam were twin witches. T*Witches, they'd dubbed themselves when they'd found each other. Which was exactly one year ago today. July Fourth. For them, Independence Day had turned into codependence day . . . linking them inescapably together. Well, happy anniversary to us.

Cam was taken aback by the bitterness of her thoughts and relieved that Alex was probably too preoccupied to have heard them.

Snap out of it, she scolded herself, determined to focus on balancing two flimsy cardboard trays filled with a half-dozen 'dogs, drinks, and Cheez Doodles. With a little bit of magick — in this case, focusing on and freezing the drinks so they wouldn't splash — she could do this.

And she would have, except she didn't.

On this muggy summer night, Camryn got the chills. An icy wind spiraled around her, as if she were in the eye of a tornado. She shivered. Goose bumps rippled along her arms, her brow grew fevered, and her eyes stung. The beach and everyone on it became one huge blur, and her head pounded.

Classic symptoms. A premonition was knocking at her door. She had no choice but to let it in. *It,* and the bad thing it would foretell.

Cam neither saw nor felt the trays of snacks slip out of her hands. What she saw instead was a trio of scrawny boys . . . about nine or ten years old . . . crouching in an empty field . . . two of them staring at the longhaired kid in the middle.

He was holding it too close. A firecracker. In a minute, he would light it. Cam could see the firecracker exploding . . . in the boy's hands.

It was an injury so intense, Cam could feel it. Was feeling it. Radiating from her hand, gripping her bicep like a tourniquet pulled too tight. Her vision had played out like a silent horror film. Only now there was a sound track.

"What do you think you're doing?" a guy growled at her. "You spill two trays of food on us, and you just stand there like a zombie?"

His friend shouted, "Whoa, stop, man. Maybe she's sick. You sick?"

Cam was wrenched out of her dream state. Enough, at least, for her to realize that she should be apologetic, offer to clean up. She couldn't. Her head pounded, her mind raced. As fast as she could, she sprinted away. Where were those boys? Could she stop the inevitable from happening? Could she do it on her own?

With her senses as her only compass, Cam ran along the seawall, kicking up sand, dodging people, blankets, food, and beach balls. Like a thoroughbred, she leaped over fences, carelessly repeating "sorry, sorry, sorry" as she ran. The fireworks show was gearing up for the big finale. No one tried to stop her. She raced toward the far end of the wall, skidding to a halt when she heard the high-pitched voices of young boys, taunting, teasing, challenging.

"Come on, man, whatcha scared or something?"

"Light it! Dude, you da man. Do it!"

"Don't rush me. . . ." the boy with the firecracker said.

Over the seawall, she saw them. Just as in her premonition, they were kneeling in an empty lot thick with weeds. But they were farther away than she'd pictured, too far for her to reach them in time.

Her eyes zeroed in on the trio. *Look up,* she willed. *Look at me*. But all three were concentrating on the explosives the middle boy was grasping. He was littler than his friends; his hands, small and brown, were shaking. The bigger kid on his left was holding a box of matches. The boy on the other side was reaching for them, ready to light the ill-fated firework.

If he'd looked up, caught her eye, Cam could have stunned him with a glare, immobilized him long enough for her to sprint over and grab the matchbox and the firecracker. But he didn't. None of them even glanced at her.

She wished Alex were there to use her gift of telekinesis. Her sister could make things move just by concentrating on them. She could *will* an object into action. Even at this distance, Als could probably have focused on the firecracker and sent it soaring toward the sea.

Where was she? Cam had heard her thoughts before; maybe her twin wasn't too far away. Quickly, she sent out a mental SOS . . . and continued racing toward the boys, waving her arms and shouting, "Stop! Stop! Don't do it! You're gonna blast off your fingers!"

On the upside, they heard her and turned. On the downside, her warning only made them act more quickly. One kid nudged the other. "Hurry up, man, do it before she can stop us."

"How's she gonna do that?" the kid in the middle countered.

Their arguing bought Cam a few minutes. But for what? She was Cam without a plan. Half of a dream team. Useless without Alex. Panic seized her.

CHAPTER TWO
AN EXPLOSIVE SITUATION

The boys were huddled together, more determined than ever to light the firecrackers. Their backs to Cam, they were totally unaware that one of them was faulty and that it would not go shooting into the sky but would explode in the hand holding it.

Cam began to tremble. What could she do on her own?

The answer lay in the spot between her collarbones. There her sun charm hung on a thin gold chain. The charm — a powerful amulet forged before her birth by the father she and Alex had never known — had begun to vibrate. But Cam was shaking so hard she'd barely noticed it. Now she could feel it trembling, growing warm against her fear-chilled skin. She gripped the delicate, hammered-gold charm and, as Alex would have, she squeezed her eyes shut and pictured the unlit firecracker, imagined it spiraling out of the boy's hands and landing safely in the water.

An incantation came to her. It was not the polished sort of spell their guardian witch, Ileana, might have used. But surprisingly it *was* as good as anything Cam had ever composed with her songwriter sister. Accepting the words as a gift of her sun charm, she desperately recited: *To foolish children let no harm come . . . Innocent they are, though willful and dumb . . . Take the danger from their hand . . . Hurl it into the sea at my command.*

Sudden panicked cries made her heart lurch, her stomach fall. She had failed. Why else would the boys be shrieking?

Terrified, Cam forced her eyes open and saw the trio tumbling backward as if they'd been propelled by a fierce wind. Scattered and screaming, they toppled end over end, crushing the tall grass as they rolled through it. She saw the streaking red trail above them . . . the tail of an unlit firecracker zooming seaward, soaring harmlessly against the darkening sky.

Safe, the shaken kids scrambled to their feet. Panting, crying, they fled across the field. The smallest one stopped and turned to stare at Cam, his eyes wide with awe and alarm.

"Run!" one of his friends hollered back to him. "Look what she did! She's a witch! Get away from her!"

She's a witch! The cry echoed in the sudden stillness.

You'd better believe it, Cam thought, collapsing as the air rushed out of her. She'd done it. She'd been needed and she'd succeeded! Maybe, she mused, gasping for breath, this was the universe's way of saying, "You can do it on your own. All by yourself, girl. Without help. Without Alex."

"Oh, please, David, we deserve a vacation, and this just fell into our laps. It's serendipity."

The voice, honeyed, cajoling, belonged to Emily Barnes, Cam's adoptive mom. "We got these tickets for free. We can't let them go to waste."

Cam had opened the door but not yet stepped inside her house. She was just about to barge in and echo her support for that idea. There'd be a family vacay after all! Her night kept on getting better.

Or not. Her dad's rejoinder stopped her. "But Cam and Alex will be alone," David Barnes, good-guy lawyer, argued.

"Cam *and* Alex," Emily pointed out. "They'll have each other. They're good kids and together they're . . . fantastic, unstoppable."

Unstoppable? Oh, yeah. Cam almost snorted. Out of the mouths of clueless moms, she thought.

Emily Barnes knew nothing of the twins' real heritage, not even their birth names — Apolla, for the sun god, and Artemis, her moony sister, Alex. David, on the other hand, had been chosen as a protector for Cam and knew more about the girls than his wife.

More, but not much.

"They're only fifteen, Em," he protested.

"Closer to sixteen," she reminded him gently. "Oh, David, how often does this kind of thing happen? Dylan's away at camp and the girls — they're smart and sensible. They'll be fine and you know it. This is a golden opportunity —"

"What golden opportunity?" Cam decided to reveal herself.

Momentarily surprised, Emily peered at Cam through her light fringe of bangs, then smiled, as she almost always did at the sight of her daughter. "Your dad and I were offered free tickets for a Mediterranean cruise. We'd only be away for three weeks —"

"And?" Cam said, trying to ignore the hollow feeling yawning in her gut again.

She wouldn't even have them around. They were both staring at her now, two pairs of questioning eyes, Emily's sky blue and Dave's deeper indigo. Did they want her approval? Her blessing?

"Sure, you should go," she said, summoning as much enthusiasm as she could. "I'll — we'll be fine."

Emily whirled to face Dave again, beaming.

Cam left them and, gripping the banister, pulled herself up the stairs. Self-pity threatened to engulf her. Alex and Cam would be together — only not. There was the Cade factor. He'd factor into every spare moment Alex had. Cam's friends were about to scatter. Her brother, Dylan, was probably hang gliding or windsurfing or skateboarding right now at Camp Extreme. And soon, her parents would set sail on the *Love Boat*.

Unless she scoured the nabe, hoping for premonitions, she'd be adrift for the summer. No one needed her here. That was for sure.

Upstairs in the room she now shared with Alex, Cam made a beeline for her laptop. Flipping on her e-mail, she bypassed the address everyone knew: cambie@mb.com and hit "Switch Screen" to another address. It was her secret screen, the one she used to communicate with one person only. Someone who did need her.

*　　*　　*

Cam had met Shane Wright last year. Met *and* fallen for him. Who wouldn't? He was buff, blond, bewitching . . . and bad.

She had to keep reminding herself of that. Bad as in a bad guy, selfish guy, *dangerous* guy. Warlock guy.

Shane was capable of using his witchy gifts in service of evil. Hadn't Cam seen it happen? Hadn't she and Alex been on the receiving end of his tricks and treachery?

Shane lived on Coventry Island, the mystical, windswept island where Cam and Alex had been born. And where they still had family. Including, they'd only recently found out, their biological mother, Miranda DuBaer.

The little island abounded with family, friends . . . and foes, Cam reminded herself.

Not so long ago, Shane was among them. An enemy.

He'd hooked up with a sketchy crowd. He'd followed the wrong leader. But he'd confessed, owned all his bad. He was ready; he wanted to reform. He needed Cam to help him do the 180.

Shane's e-mails were as startling and irresistible as he was. *I never realized how close I was to the edge, to spending my life serving evil, the opposite of our purpose as witches,* he'd written. *And then I met you, and you showed me. I am here to help, to heal, to use my*

knowledge of the craft for others, not for selfish reasons.

Cam hadn't responded at first — but her silence didn't deter him. It was understandable if she couldn't forgive him, he acknowledged. He wasn't sure he even deserved forgiveness. The enormity of the wrong he'd done perhaps was unforgivable. It would be okay if she never wrote back.

The wrong he'd done *had* been enormous. Shane had played her. He had won her trust and then betrayed her so recklessly it had almost cost her and Alex their lives.

But his e-mails were so apologetic, he seemed so miserable and hopeless that in a forgiving moment — remembering his smile, his twinkling eyes, how she didn't have to hide who she really was, how her heart danced every time she saw him — she finally did reply.

She didn't remember exactly when Shane had suggested she write back to him on a screen no one knew or could access. Nor when he'd first started urging her to return to Coventry. But a week ago, he'd written.

You are everything I want to be. Can be. I need you, Cam. Please come back to the island . . . to me. Even for a little while. Can you find it in your heart to believe me? To believe in me?

He wanted forgiveness, redemption.

Tonight, Cam thought, she was of a mind to give it to him.

In person.

Alex knew nothing of this clandestine correspondence. If she had, Cam's spiky-haired twin would have gone ballistic. Cam could hear it now: "How could you? After what he did? Ever hear the expression, 'Those who forget are doomed to repeat'?"

Cam hadn't forgotten any of it. But Alex didn't understand. In spite of everything that had gone down, she still had strong feelings for Shane. He wanted forgiveness.

"Who wants forgiveness?"

Startled, Cam jumped. "Wanna give me some warning when you're eavesdropping?" she huffed at her sister, quickly shutting down her computer.

Alex shrugged and raked her dyed locks with black-painted fingernails. "I wasn't eavesdropping," she blithely announced. "Technically, I shouldn't be able to. You should've sensed me coming up the stairs and closed your private e-mail down before I showed up."

"Why are you home so early anyway?" Cam demanded defensively. "Don't you and Cade have lots of catching up to do?"

Alex plopped down on her bed and kicked off her

scuffed mocs. "Take the sarcasm down a notch, okay? I thought I was being unselfish. I wanted to make sure you were all right."

"Why wouldn't I be?"

Alex tapped her forehead. "Post-premonition pounding? Major headache. Wanted to see if you were okay."

"So you knew." Cam smiled, trying not to gloat. "I saved a kid from getting his fingers blown off." Arms crossed, she leaned back in her swivel chair.

"You da witch," Alex said.

"Als . . . you know what? I think I'm getting some hyperhearing of my own. I heard those kids from way far off."

"Mad props." Her twin applauded lazily.

"And first time ever? I did it alone." Cam snapped her fingers and drew an imaginary victory arc in the air.

"Not to take the 'umph' out of your triumph, but that's not quite the way it went down."

"Translation?" Cam asked.

Peeling off her hooded sweatshirt, Alex said, "We, you and me, T*Witches Unstoppable, Inc. *We* intervened and saved the kid."

Cam's face grew hot with barely contained annoyance. "How do you figure? I sent a message. You didn't respond."

"Didn't I?" Alex arched her eyebrows — purple to-day, to match her hair. "Why do you think your sun charm started to buzz and vibrate?"

"You're taking credit for that?" Cam was astounded.

"I heard your telepathic shout-out. Only I wasn't close enough to get there in time. So . . . preserving my well-deserved rep as the quick-thinking twin, I tried something new. Hanging on to my amulet —" Alex demonstrated as if she were doing a show-and-tell proj-ect for a remedial class. Holding her gold half-moon charm in front of her sister's reddening face, she zipped it back and forth on its chain. "I sent you an awesome incantation — if I do say so myself. And? It worked. Eureka!"

Cam had had it. "No, *you* reek-a," she shot back. "Or your explanation does, anyway. I don't believe you."

"Whoa, petulant much?" Alex imitated Cam-slang.

Surprised at the acidy lump in her throat and its sudden companion, salty tears, Cam turned away, trying to hide her face.

When had she turned into a crybaby, a vulnerable, lonely loser? Where was Winner Cam, the stylish and so-cial soccer star everyone looked up to? She so hated feel-ing helpless.

Clearly Alex had not expected the sob-fest. She crossed the room and began gently massaging Cam's shoulders. Which made Cam feel even worse. It took everything she had not to shrug off Alex's sympathetic touch. Self-pity was bad; *being* pitied was off-the-charts worse.

"We worked together, but you really own this one. You sensed it first." Alex was backpedaling. "It was your premonition, Cam. If I had been there instead of you, those kids would have been in big trouble. Remember, I don't get premonitions."

Much later, when Cam closed her eyes, it wasn't visions of victory, or fireworks, or even Shane playing in her head. It was a verdant landscape, a calm place . . . a woman in a lavender cape, her hair twisted in a long auburn braid, whispering . . . what? Cam strained to hear. . . .

CHAPTER THREE
THE HIDDEN DOOR

"Golden slumbers fill your eyes . . . And I will sing you a lullaby . . ."

Someone was singing, stroking her hair. The light touch drifted to her cheek, tracing her cheekbones. She was a child again, safe, secure.

A breathy voice whispered, "You can't imagine how happy it makes me that you came to visit. Can you hear my heart racing?"

"Alex is the one with the hyperhearing," Cam mumbled drowsily.

"I know which twin you are, my daughter." Miranda DuBaer, Cam's birth mother, was perched on the bed. Miranda in person matched the dream Miranda: long auburn hair braided down her back, lavender cloak and all. Beyond her mother's looming, beautiful face, Cam saw a mullioned window set deep in thick stone . . . and the gilded walls of an unfamiliar room, a room curved to fit inside an enormous rounded tower.

The soaring tower of Crailmore. Which could only mean . . . Cam was really on Coventry Island?

Had she . . . dreamed herself here? Was that possible?

Miranda smiled, a faraway look in her eyes. "You seem a little dazed, disoriented. I'm not surprised. Even on the day you were born, it took you longer to awaken than your sister."

"How long have I been here?" Cam asked, flipping over onto her back and rubbing the sleep from her eyes.

"You were exhausted when you arrived yesterday and went straight to bed. So, not very long at all."

Arrived yesterday? Cam blinked once more, and it all came back to her. She had gotten here not by magick but manipulation. Dave and Emily were away; they'd never know she was gone. As long as Alex agreed to cover for her.

Cam had told Alex the truth. She needed to go there. She wouldn't say why, which flipped Alex's skeptic switch. But when Als suggested that Cam was going only to see Shane, Cam had totally denied the charge. She claimed she simply needed some time alone with Miranda.

Cam had invited Alex to come along, but knew her twin sis would never skip town while Cade was around. So they'd made a pact. Alex would do the coconspirator thing if Cam agreed to be back well before the Barneses' return. Furthermore, Cam would contact Alex if she got into trouble.

Cam sat up and stretched luxuriously. Her eyes took in the gilded room, the sunshine pouring through the tall window, the welcoming smile on Miranda's face. Cam grinned happily. She'd been sleeping on the softest, biggest bed she'd ever seen. She was in a total comfort zone, blissed out. I was right to come here, she thought. Then it hit her. This was —

"Right," Miranda affirmed. "Your father slept in this very bed —" She ran her slender fingers over the quilt as though it might still hold her murdered husband's warmth. "When he was about your age. That's why you feel so peaceful and protected here. Aron is gone, but strong magick is still here. His magick."

"Is there some special meaning to the shape?" Aron's room, wide where the bed was, narrowed into a V at the door, like a pizza slice.

Miranda explained that the family's sleeping quarters came together to form a sacred circle. All the bedrooms connected. The doors on either side of Aron's room led to those of his brothers, Thantos and Fredo. "Your grandparents wanted their three sons to be close. This was one way of trying."

"Yet failing, epically," Cam said sarcastically. In the Super Bowl of dysfunction, it was victory DuBaer.

Cam scrambled out of bed and rushed to the window.

Crailmore was the most imposing structure on the island; the fortress had been in the DuBaer family for generations. In this generation, it was ruled by Lord Thantos, head of the family. By default — de *fault* being Uncle Fredo's. The skanky brother-with-the-fewest-marbles had murdered the twins' father — sidebar, because he thought that's what Thantos wanted him to do.

Cam did not understand why Miranda still trusted the dangerous tracker. Then she shuddered. Was the hulking black-bearded warlock nearby?

"Your uncle is away," Miranda said stiffly. "But he'll be back shortly. And you really have nothing to fear."

Startled by her mother's easy eavesdropping, Cam tried to scramble her thoughts, which at the moment were: *Ba-ap! So wrong. Try again.* Safe *and* Thantos *don't belong in the same sentence.*

Thantos. The premonition came over Cam so quickly her knees buckled. To keep from falling, and to

25

keep Miranda from realizing she might, Cam pressed down hard on the windowsill. Her vision blurred. Dizziness gave way to nausea. A sheen of perspiration swathed her. She saw a book. Its cover was of old cracked leather. . . . Inside it were pages of aged parchment . . . and a hand, a smooth, confident hand was writing on the parchment. . . . *Thantos* was the only word she could make out.

"He knows you're here," Miranda was saying as Cam's vision faded.

She held her head, which was pounding furiously, and tried to focus on her mother. "Who knows? Thantos?"

Miranda's expression was troubled. "No. The boy. The blond child, wild and untrustworthy —"

It took Cam a moment. Shane! It was Shane her mother meant. She's not gonna stop me from seeing him, she thought, panicked.

"Stop you?" Her mother seemed genuinely surprised. "No. Just be cautious around him."

"And?" Cam was waiting for the rest of it. The part Emily would have stressed: "We trust you. We know you'll use good judgment."

It didn't come.

Instead, Miranda moved on. "I wish Artemis could have come with you. I was just thinking of her. Of summoning her here." She offered a beautiful kimono to Cam.

"Aren't you happy to see me?" Cam asked, poking her arms through the robe's flowing sleeves. How shallow was she that the kimono's fabric, as soft and light as a rose petal, sidetracked her for a moment. "I mean, aren't I enough?" She quickly regrouped.

"Of course!" Miranda seemed astonished that Cam would even ask. "This is not about you not being enough. I have something to tell you —"

"Go for it," Cam urged.

Miranda shook her head. "Not now. This needs to be told to the two of you, together and face-to-face. We've planned it, Ileana and I. When she returned from her trip, we were going to come and see you."

Ileana was Cam and Alex's cousin and the guardian appointed to protect the twins, ever since the day that Aron died and Miranda suffered an emotional breakdown.

"This important thing you have to tell both of us at the same time. We were here, on Coventry, for Lord Karsh's funeral. Why didn't you tell us then?"

"Because," Miranda said gently as she headed for the door, "I didn't know it then."

Cam hadn't meant to snoop. But this was her father's room. She'd been robbed of the chance to know Aron DuBaer. This, she decided after she'd dressed, was a way to begin.

She was astonished at all the accolades, certificates, awards, and trophies her father had won when he was a boy. Cam's heart swelled with pride. Was it any wonder *she* was a winner, too? At least that was what Emily often insisted. "You're amazing. An athlete graced with brains and beauty — you're a winner, baby," her adoptive mom used to say, shaking her head in wonder. "I don't know how you do it."

Emily's praise had sometimes embarrassed Cam. Now she thought maybe her gifts were not something she'd done, but a wonderful genetic legacy from this amazing man.

Aron had been an idealistic young warlock. Awarded a special citation for being the youngest ever to complete initiation, he had written of his goals: to use his talents, and the family inheritance, to help the world's people. Cam kept only one souvenir, a note Aron had scrawled, which she found in a dresser drawer: *An' it harm none, do what you will.*

Her uncles' rooms told different stories. Fredo, the youngest, had papered his walls with posters of monsters, Godzilla-sized lizards, giant rattlesnakes. Inside his desk drawer were letters from instructors and private tutors urging him to try harder. One memo struck an eerie chord. "Fredo is easily led. We must encourage him to think for himself."

Oldest brother Thantos's room was a self-obsessed braggart's den. Its theme was mirrors. Cam counted seven of different sizes and shapes on the walls, closet doors, atop his desk, and on the bureau. Even as a child, Thantos was his own biggest fan.

He did admire Aron, though — if you believed imitation the sincerest form of flattery. Cam chuckled at the number of items in his room labeled PROPERTY OF ARON DUBAER — from a bag of crystals to a spell book, even homework. It was easy to see where Aron's name had been crossed out and replaced by Thantos's. One instructor wasn't fooled. *Thantos has been copying Aron again,* was scrawled in red ink across a theme paper.

Cam could barely wait to share this stuff with Alex.

She was about to head back to her room when a picture caught her eye. She lifted the framed snapshot of three boys — tall, stout Thantos, athletic, smiling Aron, little Fredo with his head down, squinting in the sun. Cam ran a finger over her father's handsome young face. Returning the photo to its place, she accidentally hit a silver hairbrush that had been next to it. With a discomfiting clatter, the brush fell behind the dresser.

She was on her hands and knees, peering under the furniture, when she saw something odd and out of place. Inching the dresser away from the wall, she discovered a strange hatch, a door about four feet high, one that a child might go through. But why was it hidden? She reached to open it —

"Camryn, are you dressed yet?" Miranda called from the hallway.

Cam felt like a thief caught in the act. She quickly pushed the bureau back into place and bolted through the door that linked Thantos's room to Aron's.

"You've got male," her mother quipped, knocking and then entering Aron's room again a moment after Cam got there. "That's spelled m-a-l-e."

Shane! Cam's heart leaped.

Miranda stood back and allowed Cam to dash past her. "Please," her mother's soft voice called after her, "be careful."

Cam promised she would.

But she wasn't.

CHAPTER FOUR
KISS, INTERRUPTED

Be careful.

No one had to warn Alex. She'd been telling herself just that since Cade had come loping back into her life. Don't get in so deep that you can't get out. Leave an emotional escape hatch. Do not — she pictured road signs as she pedaled her bike — yield, let your defenses down. Do not let him get to you. Do not expose your heart. It's too —

"Earth to Alex —"

— Fragile. Too late. *Kaboom,* she'd already fallen.

Cade was riding beside her, their wheels, Alex noted, rotating in sync. "If I were a mind reader —" he said, with a mischievous twinkle in his black-lashed blue eyes.

Alex gripped the handlebars tightly.

"— I would know why you've got that determined look on your face. Why your eyebrows are knit in concentration, your lips pursed. Why we're biking side by side, yet you haven't heard a word I've said."

He'd been *talking* to her? Hyperhearing girl? "Oh, man," she moaned, "my bad."

"Nah," he contradicted. "There's nothing bad about you —"

She turned away. Not so he wouldn't see her blush. To stop the free fall she was in.

Alex had met Cade Richman last semester, when they'd been the new kids at Marble Bay High. They connected in many ways. There was insta chemistry and language arts — they totally got each other. There was also biology, *if* that could be measured by just one kiss. But not enough history. Cade's dad had gotten transferred to Paris; the family had to move.

Cade had packed a souvenir: Alex's heart.

Fast-forward. The boy with the dark curly hair, cobalt-blue eyes, and lopsided grin was back. All she knew was that Cade's dad had gotten him a job and a place to crash — with his boss's family. But was he here for a summer cameo or for good? The question hung in the air between them. Unasked, unanswered.

"We're almost there," she announced. She was taking Cade to a special spot, a place where wonderful things had happened. It was just a grassy field surrounding an ancient elm tree, but it was the highest point in Mariner's Park and offered a breathtaking view of Marble Bay's harbor.

Her sister had been drawn to it years ago but had never taken anyone there until Alex came to live with her. Months later, the twins had met their biological mother for the first time, there, under the huge old elm.

Alex hadn't planned on sharing it with anyone else.

But the best things in life are the unplanned ones. Like Cade.

"I see why you like it here," he said after she'd stopped and laid her bike down in the grass. Leaning his bike against the tree, he shaded his eyes to check out the boats in the distant harbor. "It's like a postcard, a snapshot of some other world." He paused, listened. "It's so different up here. Quiet, you know? Peaceful."

He got it. Alex knew he would. She felt herself swaying and her emotional safety net falling away. She'd brought a blanket, but was afraid to sit down next to him. What if she never wanted to get up? What if she got lost in his eyes, in his embrace, and couldn't find her way back?

Alex wouldn't allow it to happen. She plunged her hands into her pockets, as if that would keep her from reaching for him. In the right side of her camouflage jacket her fingers found a sharp-edged stone. It began to heat up at her touch. She knew at once that it was a crystal of pink quartz that she and Cam had used in the past to cast spells and practice magick.

She could use it now, Alex reasoned, use it to quiet her emotions and protect her heart, to keep at a distance if not Cade then her own dangerous feelings.

No. The beloved warlock Karsh, who'd given her the crystal, had taught that magick was to be used to promote love and healing, not to hide from it. She let go of the stone, hoping anyway that some of its power had entered her heart through her hand.

Alex wasn't hungry but deliberately opened her backpack and withdrew a pile of plastic containers. She'd prepared lunch — salad, tuna, cheese, bread, fruit, chips, and bottled water.

Cade whistled in appreciation. "That's what's so cool about you. You're unpredictable. Not what people expect —"

Alex stopped what she was doing and folded her arms. "Let's see, purple hair, black nail polish, a camo jacket instead of cashmere — that renders me unable to make a sandwich? That what you mean?"

"Busted," he admitted sheepishly, blushing a little.

"It's my suburban sister who's totally kitchen phobic. That girl thinks adding strawberries to Special K is gourmet cooking. Speaking of walking contradictions — looked into a mirror lately?"

Cade was the kid who'd come to school looking rough, raggedy, small-town. Nothing to suggest the well-traveled, rich boy Cade Richman was. "I never did ask you," Alex gave voice to her thoughts. "Why'd you hide who you really were?"

He leaned over on his elbow. Their faces were inches apart. "I didn't. This is who I really am. You were the only girl who ever bothered to find out. Besides, we all have secrets —"

"Not me," Alex lied. "I'm an open book. Ask me anything."

He did. Which is how they spent the hours, talking, laughing, trading stories, realizing how little — yet how much — they knew about each other. Even leaving out the witch part, Alex felt like she could talk to him forever. And listen, too.

Cade's dad was some big muckety-muck in a global conglom, and the family moved often. In his sixteen-plus years, Cade had gone to as many schools. He'd finished his sophomore year in Paris. "The city of light, they call it. It's cool, but not the perfect city people dream of."

Alex had never dreamed about Paris. Her desires had been more modest. She'd wanted to understand her own weirdness. She'd yearned to move out of the tin trailer she'd shared with her adoptive mother, Sara. And most of all, she'd wanted Sara to regain her health, beat cancer.

Two of her wishes had come true. It was the third, the one that hadn't, that would always gnaw at her. With all her gifts, her powers, she had not been able to save the only mother she'd ever known or wanted from death.

"Want me to say something in French?" Cade broke in suddenly, teasing. "It *is* the language of love, after all."

It was more than flirting, and Alex knew it. He'd sensed her gloom, was trying to pull her out before she got in too deep. He was amazing.

She brightened. "*Oui.*" *Yes* was the one French word she knew.

"Okay. See if you can figure this out. *Tu es très jolie, Alex, mon petit chou,*" he said with a sly smile.

She had no clue what it meant.

Cade leaned in and cupped her chin. "It means, you are so pretty . . ."

She blushed.

"— my little cabbage head."

Alex scrunched her face and mock punched him. "I walked right into that one, didn't I?"

Cade answered by reaching over and pulling her close. "Let's see if you walk right into this."

Alex's heart began to race. She remembered what Cade's kiss felt like. She closed her eyes and leaned toward him —

This better be worth it. She'd better come through. Or I came a long way for nothing.

— and jerked her head away roughly. What the —? Was that what he'd been thinking? Alex stared hard at Cade. She was so angry, she blurted, "What better be worth it? You mean me?"

Cade was startled. "What's going on?"

Of course you. *You think I'm here to hook up with that prissy sister of yours?*

Alex sat up sharply and moved away from him. "I don't know what game you're playing —"

"Game? Alex, what's wrong? What'd I do?" Cade wanted to know.

A game? Great! How 'bout one we both know? Hide-and-seek?

She was fuming. Her face was probably beet red. What could she say? I read your mind, you imbecile? You're just playing me? Alex leaped up, ready to grab her bike and bolt.

You're IT, Alex! Find me. . . . I'll say if you're hot or cold. . . .

She grabbed the handlebars, booted the kickstand, and stopped. Those were *not* Cade's thoughts. Someone else was here. Someone powerful enough to break into her head.

"Alex, come on," Cade said anxiously. "Give me a clue — I'm lost here." He'd come up behind her and put his hands on her shoulders, about to spin her around. She whirled, beating him to it.

Her heart sank. She didn't have to read his mind. Cade's hurt and confused feelings were all over his face. She stammered, "I'm . . . I didn't mean it . . . I mean, it's not you, it's me. . . ." Alex awarded herself an A in inane babble. "I know this is weird . . . I'm acting weird, you're probably thinking . . ."

Cade searched her eyes for a clue. She had none to give. She only hoped she could come up with an explanation he'd believe and that he'd forgive her.

Oh, Alex, you're not even trying! And you, the huntress, shame, shame!

Grimly, Alex turned away from Cade and shot back a telepathic message of her own. *Whoever you are, I will find you. You'll wish I hadn't!* She scanned the landscape, wishing for her sister's zoom-lens eyesight. On her own, Alex saw nothing.

Except this. When she turned around, Cade was gone.

*   *   *

She ached to go after him, to shout, "Wait! Don't go."

How could things have gotten so messed up, so fast? Their first quality time alone was ruined. She'd make it right with Cade — as soon as she flushed out this rude intruder.

Intruder? I could be insulted. But I'm having too much fun.

Her jaw set, Alex scrambled down the hill, digging her heels into the soft, grassy earth so she wouldn't topple. Every few steps she paused, listening, thinking. Her adversary had spied on her and Cade, broken into her head. A witch for sure, but which witch? Not Camryn, nor Miranda, not even her mischievous cousin Ileana would mess with her this way.

You're overthinking this, Alex. Use your ears . . . use your instincts.

Don't tell me what to do! Alex shot back, walking faster, more deliberately. She knew this park, this view by heart. What wasn't she seeing?

Suddenly, she realized it didn't matter if she couldn't flush someone out by sight. She could hear. There was a swishing sound, like someone dragging a blanket across the grass. Then a sliding, skidding, and bump! Her mystery guest had fallen.

A memory came to her. Weeks ago on Coventry

Island, a short young witch tripped on her too-long cape and tumbled down a flight of stairs. No! It couldn't be —

Michaelina?

"Ta-da!" The teen witch, arms outspread, popped out from behind a tree and gleefully announced, "The one and only!"

Alex blinked. Oh, no! It really *was* her, the double-dealing rival Alex had met on Coventry. What was she doing here?

Michaelina, with her twinkling green eyes, mischievous mouth, and pixie-gone-punk hairdo, had been one of a trouble-brewing trio of witches who called themselves the Furies. Sersee, Epie, and Michaelina. They'd tried to kick serious T*Witch butt and almost succeeded — thanks to Mike, who had briefly befriended the twins, then led them into a near-lethal trap.

"You're not holding *that* against me," Mike quipped. "What do mainlanders say, 'Bygones —'"

"In your case, it's *be gone*. Now would be a good time," Alex snapped.

Michaelina smiled big. "You haven't changed at all. That's good."

"What are you doing here?" Alex fingered her moon charm menacingly.

Michaelina held up mini-palms. "I come in peace. Just to check out mainland life. It's as simple as that —"

Jaw set, Alex demanded, "Who sent you?

"No one! Look, Alex, I know what happened was bad. I learned a lesson, too. I'm not one of Sersee's servants anymore — I . . . I know this sounds sappy, but I'm sorta trying to figure it out, y'know? Looking for a second chance?"

"At what? Another betrayal? What makes you think I wouldn't put a spell or curse on you?"

"No way." Michaelina snorted. "You're a card-carrying member of Witches Magnanimous. You totally believe that hooey, 'that all things might grow to their most bountiful goodness.' It's not in your nature to hurt me."

Mike was right, but for the wrong reason. Alex wasn't angry enough to hurt the girl. It was something in the sprite's eyes, the way she put up this totally tough front. It reminded Alex of someone.

It was the way she might have ended up had the beloved warlock Karsh not brought her to Cam.

CHAPTER FIVE
CAM'S MISSION

Shane had come for her. And just like that, her rational mind closed down and her rash heart opened up. Cam did not demand the explanation Shane owed her. She did not demand the cautiousness she owed herself. She forgot about Jason. She forgot about Shane's betrayal. His arms were outstretched. She knew she'd rush into them.

The massive mahogany doorway of Crailmore, meant to humble those who passed through it, did not diminish Shane Wright. It framed him, as if he were a princely portrait. He was almost posed, it struck Cam, his hands on his hips, legs astride, shiny blond hair brushing his broad shoulders. His eyes, blue as a cloudless sky, searched her face.

Her skilled gray eyes glazed over; her heart was in her throat. Fluttering butterfly wings invaded her stomach, only to settle the moment he closed his arms around her.

Playing it cool was not an option. Not when Shane was so hot.

"You're here," was all he said, holding her tightly and sighing with relief. Had he doubted she would come? Shane brushed away her bangs and kissed her lightly on her forehead. "Come with me," he whispered.

No way. Not until you offer up some real explanation for your betrayal. Not until you tell it to my face, to my mother's face. I'm not going anywhere with you until you prove to both of us you've changed.

Okay. That's what Cam should have said.

Only, how could she? His hand closed over hers and their fingers entwined naturally. They walked silently down the steps, along the walkway, and through the iron gates that surrounded the mansion.

She'd been so wrapped up in him that Cam hadn't noticed the black horse, sleek and huge, tethered to one of the fence spikes. Shane pulled her toward it, but Cam shied back. "What is that?" she asked without thinking.

Shane laughed. "That is a stallion," he explained proudly, reaching up to stroke its dark, silky mane.

In theory, Cam considered herself a friend to all creatures great and small, but when the really big ones got so up close and personal that their hot breath warmed your face and stirred your hair . . . "friendship" ended there.

"This is Epona," Shane was saying, stroking the immense beast's snout. "He looks fierce, but he wouldn't hurt a fly."

"How's he feel about humans?" Cam asked.

Epona was ink black, from his nervously flicking tail to his frighteningly alert eyes. Evil and angry looking, they seemed almost to be taking her measure. She wanted to turn away, but Shane's arms were around her shoulders now, moving her gently closer to the stallion.

"Make friends with him." Shane guided her hand across the horse's neck. It was taut, muscular, and rough as burned weeds. "He's our ride to the beach. Aren't you, boy?"

"Can't we walk?" In the brief time Cam had spent on Coventry, she'd walked everywhere. So had everyone else.

Shane shook his head. "Too far."

"And cars are —?"

"Too mainland."

"So, skateboard, Rollerblades, scooters, bus, train, Learjet . . . ?"

"Horses," he told her, "played an important part in our history. Black ones, like him, symbolized power and vitality. No one taught you about that? You never heard the name Epona before?"

"That would be a no. And no," Cam answered.

"I'll teach you, then. Give me your foot." Shane laced his hands together and held them out for her to step into. Which she did, reluctantly. He placed her sneakered foot into the stirrup. "Up you go. Hold on to the saddle horn. I won't let you get hurt. Trust me."

A rebellious thought crept from its corner. Trust? Déjà vu, anyone? Sequel-itis? This boy has lied to you before. You trusted him, and he betrayed you.

He read her mind with ease. "Cam, you've come all this way," he said, his eyes innocent and clear. "Don't give up on me now."

Embarrassed, she squirmed in the saddle and, when Shane hoisted himself up behind her, his arms encircling her waist, she told her instincts to relax.

The young warlock held Epona to a slow pace as they trotted through the countryside surrounding Crailmore and then into the deep woods behind the estate.

They were headed to Coventry's north shore. Shane told her, "It's usually pretty deserted, since there are no beaches or ferry docks."

"The shore less traveled?" Cam teased. She couldn't tell if he'd smiled or not at her poetry reference.

"Really," he continued, "you should see it. After all, you own it."

"I what?" Cam looked over her shoulder at him.

"All this" — he nodded straight ahead as they emerged from the woods toward a rocky shore — "this is all DuBaer property. It's yours."

"No," she corrected, "it belongs to Thantos."

"Your uncle," Shane pointed out.

"Unfortunately," she mumbled.

They'd ridden as far as they could take the horse, stopping near the edge of a steep drop-off. Dismounting, they left the animal on flat ground and headed, hand in hand, down a rocky slope, balancing precariously on the sharp edges of rock, formed by decades of wind and mist rising off the Great Lake.

Cam, a natural athlete, turned out to be more agile than Shane. She took the lead a few times and helped him negotiate the rocky sea-battered terrain. It was cooler and windier on this part of the island, and Cam was glad for the scrunchie in her pocket. Once the hair was out of her eyes, she looked around. The view was spectacular. Lake Superior stretched before them, the midday sun glistening on its wind-rippled surface.

"Thanks for coming." Shane squeezed her hand lightly as they walked along the shore. "I'm so glad, so grateful you're here."

Don't make me regret it, the rebel brain cell piped up again. "Everyone deserves a second chance," Cam said lightly. "Though in your case, it's kind of a third chance."

"There's no excuse for what I did," the blond warlock said confidently, almost as if he'd rehearsed it. He brushed a hank of windblown hair off his forehead. "I gained your trust and led you to Sersee, who tried to kill you. There's no pretty way of saying that."

She didn't remind him of the time before that, when he'd used her best friend Beth to trick her. That time, he had been working for Thantos.

"All I can do is try and get you to understand me," he was saying. "I hope you'll forgive me. I'm not that guy anymore. I don't work for Thantos, and Sersee and I are over."

They walked; he talked. Every so often, Shane picked up a stone and hurled it into the water, breaking the sheen of its surface. Cam didn't interrupt. Maybe if he kept going, she could bring herself to believe that, this time, he was telling the truth.

"It was despicable, unconscionable," Shane continued. "I was lost, morally. It's really hard when you have all these gifts, all these powers, and no guidance about how to use them."

Cam knew that Shane's parents, followers of Thantos, had kicked him out when he renounced his loyalty to the terrible tracker. She was about to ask why he hadn't gone to Lord Karsh, or any of Coventry's Exalted Elders, most of whom knew Thantos's flaws. "But why —" She got that far, when he whirled suddenly, his blue cloak billowing.

"Watch this," he cut short her question. From the leather pouch on his belt he pulled a handful of green leaves and purple berries. Mumbling an incantation, words lost in the sea wind, he tossed the herbs into the turbulent air, which carried them to the cliff where Epona was tethered.

Above them, the great horse shied and whinnied pitifully. And then his sweat-sheened black body began to change color. His legs turned green, his body gold, and his mane a crimson red.

"Do you recognize him now?" Shane challenged.

Cam didn't. All she saw was a shivering horse beginning to froth at the mouth. "Please change him back," she begged.

Shane stared at her for a second, his eyes searching hers. "Can't you do it?" he asked.

Cam clasped her necklace. It was cold and still. No warmth trembled through it; no spell came to mind. "No," she admitted. "Please, Shane."

He put his arm around her, enfolded her now-chilled body in the soothing heat of his cloak. So quickly that anyone with eyes less talented than Cam's might have missed it, Shane reached inside his shirt and grasped a crystal horseshoe-shaped medallion that had been hidden there, secured around his neck by a leather thong. This time he made no attempt to muffle his incantation.

"Powers of sea, sky, and land," Shane called into the wind, *"release this creature at my command. Return him to black, tall and tame. Hide the bright form in which he came."*

It was a mystifying spell. Cam had no idea what it meant, but Epona's misery ended. The horse stood calm again, black, tall, and tame, as Shane had ordered.

"What was that?" Cam asked, shaken but impressed. "What did you mean about the 'form' in which he came? Where did he come from?"

Again, Shane's blue eyes scoured her face. And when he was satisfied that she really didn't know the answer, he said, "From the sea, according to legend. I mean, all the horses on the island were supposed to have come from the sea. I don't remember the whole story. Probably swam ashore from a stranded ship or something."

Cam glanced again at the huge animal. He snorted and pawed the earth above them. "I never heard that incantation before —" she told Shane, studying Epona, looking for a trace of the bold colors he'd displayed only moments before.

"It's pretty basic," he said, quickly changing the subject. "Cam, I've made such a mess of my life, misused the powers I was blessed with —"

She looked at him.

"None of what I told you is a real excuse," Shane said. "I'm ashamed to say I just followed along, first with Thantos, then with Sersee. Then I met you. That's when I knew for sure that I had to change. But by then, I was too deeply entrenched. I'm so, so sorry, Cam."

Cam felt herself tearing up. Her heart went out to him, to the little lost boy he'd been, battered, betrayed, booted from his home. Maybe she'd sensed that all along. Maybe that's why her feelings toward him defied reason.

Shane covered her hands with his and looked into her eyes. *Maybe we're soul mates.*

Cam's eyes widened. Had she done it? Read someone's mind who wasn't related to her? "Were you just thinking . . . ?"

Shane blushed, and Cam had her answer. She was developing higher skills. On her own. Something else hit her. She'd not thought about Jason since she got here.

Maybe it was meant to be. Maybe Jason had to leave so she could see her way clear to Shane.

Cam had not been lying when she'd told Alex she needed to come to Coventry to see if Shane had been sincere about doing a 180. But there was a greater good, a higher purpose. She knew it now. Her mission as a witch was to heal, to help, to be sure all things — did that not include people? — might grow to their most bountiful goodness.

Shane needed her.

"I do, Cam. You have no idea how much." He'd read her mind again. He wrapped his arms around her and pulled her toward him into the warm shelter of his cloak.

As she closed her eyes to receive his kiss, his crystal horseshoe pendant brushed her sun charm and produced a strange and startling shock.

A real buzzkill.

Cam returned to Crailmore late in the day. She found Miranda in the herb garden. Her mother had traded her flowing cape for more practical overalls and a broad-brimmed straw hat to shield her face from the afternoon sun. She heard her daughter's approach and greeted her with a smile.

Which Cam returned one hundredfold.

Miranda's heart quickened. Her daughter — one of

the two precious children she'd once thought were lost to her forever — was so beautiful, so radiant in her unconcealed joy. "Things went well," she ventured.

"It was unbelievable." Cam couldn't stop smiling.

"Tell me all about it," her mother urged. "Here." She handed Cam a trowel and a small pot in which a delicate pale green shoot grew. "You can help me. I'm putting in some new lavender."

In Marble Bay, Cam had never gardened. The Barnes' family hired landscapers for that. But right now she felt she could do anything. She was overflowing with energy . . . and love. She took the tool Miranda handed her and absentmindedly hugged the little terra-cotta pot while recalling her wonderful day.

Her words tumbled out in a seemingly endless stream. She explained the cruel circumstances that had led Shane astray and confided how desperately he wanted to reform. She wondered if Miranda might help him. He was such a misunderstood boy and needed so much to be loved and accepted.

Miranda smiled and nodded and expressed not a word of doubt until Cam mentioned the horse.

"His name is Epona. Shane said that horses are an important part of our heritage —"

Miranda looked up from the fragrant lavender seedling she was transplanting. "Epona?" She brushed the dirt off her hands and faced her daughter, trying to disguise her alarm. "A red horse?" she asked.

"No, he's totally black. But Shane was trying to impress me and he put a spell on —"

"Did he come from the sea?" Miranda interrupted.

"The horse?" Cam shrugged. "In a way, I guess. Shane said all the horses on the island . . ." She let it trail off. Miranda seemed suddenly upset. "What happened? What's wrong?" Cam urged.

"Nothing," her mother insisted. "The heat of the day. I've been out here since . . . early afternoon."

"It's about Epona, isn't it?" Cam guessed. "He was a little high-strung at first, but he settled down quickly. It was okay. I'm fine."

But even as she tried to reassure her mother, a wave of nausea rocked her. Her head began to pound. The pounding became the sound of a horse's hooves galloping toward her. Instead of Epona, it was a red horse that came charging. His body was wet with sea foam and as he approached, his coat bled into the strange colors of Shane's spell. His wild mane remained red but his legs grew green and his body a translucent gold. . . .

"The death horse galloping out of the sea," Miranda was saying. Cam didn't know how long she'd been lost in her vision, but her mother was standing now, looking troubled. "In legends, he is sometimes red, sometimes black, and sometimes strangely colored. His mission was to pull the chariot of the sun god across the sky each day."

The sun god. Apollo. The one she'd been named for, the one that held the key to her earliest powers.

"And then to carry the dead across the water —"

Cam squinted up at her mother, trying to understand what Miranda was talking about.

"But perhaps your friend didn't know that particular legend. And, of course, they're not all about death and chaos. There are so many tales and myths of the magical power of horses," her mother quickly backpedaled. "Stallions tamed are said to become talismans of strength and virility. Some believe that the imprint of a horse's footprint is a symbol of power. Another superstition has it that to possess a horseshoe is good luck, that it means you are under its protection —"

A horseshoe — like Shane's crystal pendant . . .

Miranda picked up her gardening tools and walked with Cam back to the house to get ready for dinner. As they passed through the massive doors, Cam thought she heard her mother say, "The time has come to tell them. Ileana is going to have to cut her vacation short."

"Tell who what?" Cam asked without thinking.

Miranda seemed startled. "I didn't say anything," she said.

CHAPTER SIX
BREAKING THE RULES

Alex had made a rule. She would not break into Cade's head. She wanted a real relationship with him, a normal relationship. Which meant no mind reading. Except in an emergency.

She owed the baffled boy an explanation for her bizarro behavior, something believable and forgivable. What she didn't know was exactly how freaked he was, or if he still wanted a relationship with the wacko he now probably thought she was.

The quickest way to his heart, she rationalized, was through his brain. If this didn't qualify as a 911, what did?

Immediately after promising Michaelina that she'd give the persistent pixie one last chance at friendship,

Alex had biked back to the Heights, to the imposing house where Cade was hanging for the summer.

A thirty-something woman wearing pearls with her silk sweater set and color-coordinated slacks met her at the door. "Alex?" the utter stranger said, her hand rushing to her throat as if to choke off the next line on her mind, which was, *This can't be the girl Cade has been brooding about.*

Alex looked at herself. She hadn't stopped to consider what she must look like. After two long bike rides in one humidity-drenched day, she was not a pretty sight. Her shirt was sticky with sweat. She ran a hand through her hair, confirming the worst — lavender-streaked layers were in a total tangle. As for the eye makeup she never wore — except for today when she'd raided Cam's cabinet — it had undoubtedly smeared and left her with rank raccoon eyes. Alex tried to swab away the mess, then mindlessly wiped her mascara-smudged hand on her already rancid T-shirt.

The woman at the door winced. A nanosecond later her shocked expression changed to a welcoming smile. "How rude of me. I'm Moira McDonald," she announced. "Cade's out back, on the deck. He's been quiet since he got back, but I have a feeling he's been hoping you'd show up. Why don't you come in and wash up first? I'll lend you a top."

"That'd be great," Alex said, hoping she sounded grateful. But as she followed Cade's keeper up the stairs, she wondered uneasily if the top would be silk — or worse, pink?

It turned out to be a skinny black tee, which she slipped into distractedly, because through the guest room window she spotted Cade. And Alex did what she'd told herself she wouldn't. Like a burglar listening for the clicks of a combination lock, she closed her eyes and strained to catch his thoughts.

In spite of the CD player on his lap and the headset parting his sleek black hair, the buff boy was stressing. About her! Even as she listened in she could feel her cheeks begin to burn. *Why'd she do that*, Cade was thinking. *She led me on, then freaked when I tried to kiss her. I just don't get it. Unless . . . oh, man, maybe she was really sick — a manic-depressive or something — upbeat one minute, scared and suspicious the next? She might have needed help instead of someone booking on her. I could have stayed. But what if she meant to blow me off?*

Alex abandoned her spy post and hurried down to him.

With the headset clamped in place, he hadn't heard her coming out and turned, startled, when she tapped him on the shoulder. Relief and joy played across his handsome face, followed by a quizzical look. "Insanity? That's your defense?"

Her fragile confidence crumbled until Cade pointed to the T-shirt she was wearing, the one Moira-with-the-pearls had given her. It said, INSANITY IS HEREDITARY. YOU GET IT FROM YOUR CHILDREN.

Alex managed a nervous laugh. "Would temporary insanity work for you?" she asked hopefully.

Cade's laugh was as edgy as hers. And about as desperately hopeful. He moved over and made room for her on the slatted lounge. "Listen, Alex," he began, when she sat beside him, "I probably shouldn't have bolted like that —" He reached for her hand, which she gave awkwardly, and she listened, with mingled guilt and gratitude, as he told her, practically word for word, the thoughts she'd eavesdropped on.

"I'm sorry I didn't hang around to find out what was really going on," he ended, looking at her questioningly. Expecting an explanation.

Alex desperately wanted to tell him the truth. She could practically taste the words, hear them as they tumbled from her mouth. But she said nothing.

"You got scared, was that it?" he prompted. "That's why you pulled away and acted so weird?"

"No, Cade. I wasn't scared, not really. I just . . ." Alex paused and took a deep breath. Maybe one day she'd be able to be totally honest with him. But not today, not now. And yet she didn't want lie to him, either.

She could, and did, murmur, "It won't happen again, I promise you." And when she looked up at him, he leaned toward her.

"So," she continued very softly, her voice sticking in her throat, "if you're willing to —"

"Take it from where we left off?" He finished the thought and punctuated it with a long, gentle, soulful kiss. The one she'd been remembering.

"I have a confession," Cade whispered.

"About why you really came back," Alex asked, touching her lips, which still held the memory of his and felt as if they were softly vibrating, practically purring.

"You read my mind."

"Nuh-uh, not this time," she murmured forgetfully.

He shot her a look, then smiled and explained. Months of convincing and compromising had gone into getting his dad to allow him to come back. Mr. Richman had already made plans for his son. He'd secured Cade a summer internship with a big-deal corporation head-quartered in London. The compromise for allowing Cade to return to Marble Bay started tomorrow: a nine-to-five summer gig working with his father's friend, Moira's husband, a vice president at a law firm in Boston. "My dad's got my whole life mapped out," Cade told her.

"But it's not what you want?" Alex ventured.

"I don't know what I want. Maybe I'll end up on the path he's clearing for me. But right now, I've got to figure some things out for myself." He didn't add aloud, *Like you, Alex . . . like why I needed to see you, wanted to so badly, and whether you . . . whether you feel . . . the same way.*

Hours later, tired but exhilarated, Alex accepted a lift home.

She and Cade had eaten dinner with the McDonalds and spent the evening playing Trivial Pursuit and making and devouring ice-cream sundaes. Alex had a surprisingly comfortable evening.

She and Cade pulled up to the Barneses' house just before midnight.

Cade helped get her bike off the rack on the back of the McDonalds' SUV. "I'll be off work tomorrow at five," he reminded her, "so I'll see you —"

"— at five-oh-one." Alex gave him a peck on the cheek and a big grin.

She waltzed into the house on a cloud, only to plunge to Earth again when she grabbed the ringing phone. "Where have you been?" demanded the high-strung voice on the other end.

"Uh, hi," she stammered. "Emily? Is it . . . late?"

"We've been calling for hours!" Cam's adoptive mom's panic morphed slowly into relief. "Didn't you get the messages? We left them at home and on Cam's cell phone. We were just about to call the . . ." She trailed off.

"We were really worried." Dave had taken the phone from his wife. "We thought something had happened."

"No, no, I'm . . . we're both . . . fine," Alex assured them. "Cam's . . . um . . . she just stepped into the shower."

There was silence. Then Dave, who knew of the girls' true heritage and their enthusiasm for helping and healing, gave her an out. "Were you . . . needed somewhere?" he asked softly.

"Totally," Alex concurred. "But everything's fine now."

Well, that part was true, she told herself. Cade *had* needed her. And for all she knew Cam *was* stepping into a shower . . . on Coventry Island.

"Good," Dave said. "Tell Cam we called. Everything's good here. It'll probably be easier to reach us by e-mail than phone. Ask Cam to check in, okay?"

"E-mail." Alex was on it instantly. She promised them Cam would send a message as soon she got out of the shower.

They would have received one, with Alex pretending to be her long-gone twin, only Cade called. She never made it to the computer, but fell asleep talking to him instead.

Michaelina flung open the door to her apartment before Alex knocked. "So, can I pass for a mainlander?" she demanded, twirling on toe shoes.

"Dude, you can't even pass Go," Alex informed her. Somewhere in the style wilderness of pop divas, Michaelina had gotten very, very lost. Alex was no fashionista, but she did know a disasterpiece when it was in her face. Or in this case, dancing in the doorway of a shabby attic rental apartment.

Multiply pierced and studded, Michaelina had spared no body part in her attempt — or rather, stab — at "mainlander."

A line of little hoops outlined her ear rims and perforated her left nostril; another, this one spiked like a miniature dog collar, was stuck through one eyebrow. Her thorny tattoo necklace protruded from a stretchy tank top that accented her twiglike frame. Her ankles dangled skinny and pale from pants three sizes too big. Why one leg was cuffed to the knee while the other draped her ankle was anyone's guess. Whether meant to signify hip-hop, goth, or skater-girl, the effect was nearly as over-the-top as what she'd done with, or to, her face.

Coventry Girl's makeup — including heavy black eye-liner and thick retro white lipstick — weighed almost more than she did.

All in all, Alex decided, the mainland wanna-be looked like a cross between Nightmare Barbie and a hip-hop L'il Mike.

Fists on her hips, Michaelina pouted. "Who died and left you trend queen?"

Alex shoved her hands in her jean pockets and tried to stifle a laugh. "To answer your original question, if you're trying to fit in, that would be a resounding no."

"Who said anything about fitting in? I asked if I could pass for a mainlander. I copied your look."

"You didn't copy me, you did a hostile takeover. And BTW, I don't have 'a look.'" Alex retorted.

"Are you always this grumpy in the morning?" Michaelina turned away sullenly. "There are charms to banish the morning grouchies, you know."

"Are there any to banish you?" Alex parried.

Michaelina's shoulders slumped as she faced Alex again. "I thought you'd be flattered," she muttered. "I was trying to be like you, not follow the crowd."

"Point taken," Alex conceded. "We can work with it."

The micro-witch brightened. "Come in. Check out my new place."

Alex trailed Mike into her digs, which were oddly

tepee-shaped. Daylight filtered bleakly through the only window, a slanted skylight desperately seeking a scrubbing. "It already feels like home," Michaelina proudly announced.

"So, *homes*." Alex purposely accented the word. "What are you really doing here? On the mainland, in this —"

"Hovel?" Michaelina guessed.

"You could put it that way," Alex responded.

"I never expected you, you of all witches, to diss my digs," Mike challenged. "You've changed. A lot. When did you get all trendoid?"

On the bus ride over, Alex decided, not caring whether the petite witch picked up the thought. She'd been shocked at the nabe where Mike had chosen to live. Who knew this area existed just outside the pristine Marble Bay, Mass? She was shocked, too, at her own squeamishness as the bus rolled by block after block of burned-out, boarded-up stores, rickety, run-down houses, abandoned cars, and graffiti-sprayed buildings and fences —

"Oh, and that tin-trap of a trailer you grew up in was pure luxury, right?"

Alex was taken aback. Had she ever discussed her pre–Marble Bay life with Michaelina? The canny young witch had done her fact-checking. But why?

"We all have 'before' lives, don't we?" She was smiling when Alex looked at her. "Mine would make your hair stand up — if it wasn't already spiked to the max. Truce, okay? Can I get you something?"

Alex followed the girl to the farthest corner of the narrow room — and felt as though she'd been kicked in the chest. The kitchen setup — a two-burner stove on a peeling wooden counter and a dismal mini-fridge — was almost identical to the one she'd grown up with in Montana. With Sara.

"This is a dump," Alex struck out, ignoring the lump in her throat. "But at least it's aboveground. As opposed to your old address."

"Ooooh, low blow." Michaelina pretended to be hurt.

The caves of Coventry Island, underground and undetected, had been the Furies' cold, barren hideout.

"The truth, Michaelina," Alex demanded. "Give it up —"

The petite urchin ignored her, opened the half-fridge, and stepped back so that Alex could look inside. "Uh-oh, empty."

But it wasn't empty. On the refrigerator shelf stood a jar of peanut butter, one pocked tomato, and a wilted head of lettuce. Exactly what had been in the fridge the day Alex realized that Sara was very, very ill. The same day she had first glimpsed Cam . . . Could it possibly be a coincidence? Coincidence or —

"Conspiracy?" Mike chuckled cheerfully. "Get real, Alex. You think I toted this in?" The pixie swung the fridge door shut. "What say we hike down to the deli and grab us a couple of lattes?"

Alex didn't have to be asked twice. "No more lies," she demanded after they'd traipsed down the wobbly stairs and hit daylight. "What are you doing here? What do you want?"

"What's the use? You won't believe me. You still don't trust me," the diminutive girl answered, taking two steps to keep up with every one of Alex's. "I came because I thought you were cool. And I wanted to see where and how you lived. And because there's nothing to keep me on Coventry anymore. After you and your sister skipped out, the gang sorta broke up. Epie's doing a bid in juvie. Shane's gone straight. And Sersee's licking her wounds —"

"And you?" Alex persisted.

"Me?" Mike shrugged. "Okay, coming clean? Nobody wanted me there. Not Sersee or Shane or even my own family — what was left of it."

"Meaning?"

"I'm an orphan. Or I might as well be. My moms split when me and my sibs were babies. My pops tossed me out when I was ten. Said I reminded him of Delta, that was my mother's name. Said I was nothing but trouble and never would be anything else." Michaelina looked away, but not so fast that Alex couldn't see the girl's nose getting red and her eyes misting with tears.

"So you came because —" Alex had a sudden thought. "Do you think your mom is on the mainland? Is that why you're really here?"

Michaelina was honestly perplexed. "Uh, no. Why would I do that? I like my freedom. A mommy figure isn't what I'm looking for. Okay, my turn," she piped up, completely over her emotional moment. "I get to ask you a question."

"Knock yourself out." Alex surrendered, her gray eyes sweeping the street, looking for whatever trouble might be brewing in this trouble-prone stretch of town.

"When you did sell out?"

The question startled her.

"When did you become conformo?" the pixie went on. "You grew up in a poor neighborhood, but you hate this one. You're all scared of it. You're laughing at the way I'm dressed, just the way people used to laugh at you. You put up this front of being indie girl, but you don't even want to believe I'm here on my own, doing things my way."

Alex fished for something to say. All that came out

was, "How are you affording this? Where's the coin coming from?"

"I borrowed some," Michaelina said carefully. "And I put a tiny spell on the landlord to make him think I'd be good for it. Besides, I thought I'd do the righteous mainland thing and get a job. Unless you disapprove of that, too? I mean, the Barnes are probably sharing the bling-bling with you."

Alex's back went up. She'd refused to take any more money from Cam's folks than she absolutely had to — even if they were now her legal guardians. No designer duds, no cool computer, new CDs, not even a magazine subscription. Her most prized possession was a guitar, Dylan's old one. Even her bike had been Cam's castoff.

Apparently Mike hadn't read her mind. Or wasn't interested in her defensiveness. "So when did it happen? When did you become your sister on the inside, too, instead of your own person?"

Alex's attention was suddenly diverted by a clamorous metallic sound. Three little boys were coming toward them. They were kicking a can. Their bantering voices, which she heard from far off, sounded oddly familiar, though she knew she'd never seen the boys before.

Michaelina was oblivious to the trio. "You know I'm right," she insisted. "You used to be a free spirit —"

The voices. They belonged to the kids who had been playing with fireworks on the Fourth. They were the boys she'd helped Cam save.

"When did you get sucked into playing the game by someone else's rules?" Mike nattered on. "When did you stop being *you*?"

Alex heard the question. She turned away from the ragamuffins and tried to scramble her thoughts so that Michaelina wouldn't know she'd hit a nerve.

Despite her insistence on not owing anyone anything, in the past year she'd gotten used to living well — under the Barneses' roof and rules. So what if she hadn't started dressing like Cam and her crew. Was that all that remained of her fierce independent spirit? Had she really, as Michaelina mocked, strayed so far from her roots? From the person Sara had brought her up to be?

If Sara Fielding could see her now, what would she think of Alex?

"There's the witch!" Wide-eyed and trembling, the three boys were staring at her. "She's the one from the beach. Let's get outta here!" they cried over their shoulders as they hightailed it up the street.

"What was that?" Michaelina wanted to know.

Alex tried to shrug nonchalantly. "How should I know?" she replied, to keep herself from saying what she knew to be true. *Even they think I'm my sister.*

CHAPTER SEVEN
THE SECRET PASSAGE

The hidden door behind the dresser in Thantos's childhood bedroom beckoned Cam. Despite the excitement of her amazing day with Shane, something drew her back here. She needed to find out where the strange hatch led — before she could decide if it was worth mentioning to Miranda.

Pleading exhaustion, she'd gone to bed early. In the middle of the night, when she was certain her mother was asleep, she made for Thantos's room, careful to move the dresser out of the way slowly and quietly.

The small door was unlocked and swung open easily. It opened into a murky tunnel, which Cam followed to a stone stairway. It led into the caves of Coventry

Island. She'd been there before, lured by Sersee. She wasn't scared, though, as she descended the stairs, which twisted and spiraled. The creepy quotient was definitely daunting. She'd bet Thantos used this secret chamber to torment his terrified brother Fredo.

At the bottom of the stairwell, Cam found herself in a high-ceilinged, circular cavern. Like rays from a black sun, five tunnels led off in different directions. As she stood in the center of the dark vault, a strange feeling came over her.

It was neither a vision nor a premonition coming on. She did not grow dizzy or hear the loud buzzing that usually heralded her prophecies. She simply knew something suddenly that she had no rational way of knowing.

There was a book.

She hadn't read it but somehow knew a portion of its contents. The book told of what lay beneath the soil of Coventry, what — and who — she might encounter should she journey farther, deeper into this part of the fabled caves. What kinds of inhabitants, more dangerous than the Furies, might be found. Here spirits of the dead roamed, and others, deranged souls who struck out blindly at any who dared enter. These wretched apparitions could materialize at any bend in the tunnel.

This came to her as fact without fear. Cam felt a sense of calm and peace. She'd be protected here. She didn't know why, or how, or from what exactly, but whatever had lured her here this time, that same powerful magick would not allow harm to come to her. She stood very still in the middle of the circular chamber and waited for her senses to guide her.

Her hearing, never as astute as Alex's, was the first sense awakened. She heard scratching sounds coming from one of the tunnels. She listened intently. A steady, monotonous scraping, like fingernails on a chalkboard, raised goose bumps on her arms and turned her stomach.

Yet she forged forward.

Her eyes, beacons in the dark, were on high beam. So she saw him well before he saw or sensed her. A spindly man, his cloaked back to her, was bent in concentration over a stone outcropping, a table of sorts formed by a ledge in the wall. His frayed cape had probably once been a burgundy color. Now it was threadbare and as sleek with grease as his long, stringy, dark hair, which was tied back in a rattail.

This was no apparition, no haunted spirit. What, then? Who would sit in the icy bowels of Crailmore and what was he doing?

Afraid only of startling him, she advanced slowly and stealthily.

As she drew closer, she realized what he was doing and what she had heard. With a quill pen, the hunched wretch was laboriously scrawling a message on stiff parchment. Grungy and fragile as he looked, his hand was steady on the page. A pile of already completed sheets sat at his right hand. Was he composing a book? Was it the book she'd seen in her vision this morning, the book she'd thought of a moment ago?

She was only a few feet away. Surely he would sense her presence soon. She expected him to whirl around, a withered soul, some nutcase whose lair she'd invaded. When he did spin to face her, she saw not the face of a hapless aged hermit. Smooth and unlined, this was a warlock about Shane's age. His icy expression could have been carved from the very stone he was using as a table.

She noticed, too, his hair was cropped short on top. Cam had an insane urge to tell him the mullet look was so over — but fear, the first she'd felt since sneaking through the odd door in Thantos's room, stopped her cold.

She found her voice. "Who . . . what are you . . . doing?"

The rattailed warlock did not respond. His gaze locked on Cam, pinned her with his inky eyes.

She swallowed, trying to show no fear. But just then her sun charm grew hot against her chest, so hot she thought it might burn her. When she tried to lift it, she got an electric shock.

She knew now to retreat, to run. This same force that had pulled her down into this cave was pushing her out. She heeded the warning at the exact same moment the warlock reached out to grab her. Something gleamed from the collar of his grimy shirt. As Cam raced away, she realized what she had seen. A horseshoe-shaped crystal hanging from a gold chain.

It was identical to the amulet Shane had been wearing.

"No *way*!" Shane assured her the next day. He'd come again to Crailmore to see her, to spend the afternoon together. "You think Epona is some descendant of an evil equine empire? A symbol of death?"

Death hauling sun god's chariot, Cam thought.

That'd be her. Or her namesake.

A book she'd found this morning in Crailmore's huge library confirmed Miranda's memory of the legend of Epona. How much of it did Shane know? Why would he tease her, or test her about ancient symbols of evil?

Until she had answers, Cam had decided, she would not let her feelings blind her.

She could do this now, because her senses were sharper here. Her ability to hear things from far away, while still not in Alex's league, had improved. Here on Coventry, she was more attuned, in tune, with her biological heritage. More like, she thought with a start, the girl she was born to be.

That's what she'd been thinking as she walked beside Shane along the cobblestone path leading away from Crailmore. Despite last night's encounter with the weirdo in the cave, she was feeling strong again, secure, empowered.

Which was why the sudden dizziness took her by surprise. She reached out to Shane as everything blurred. But he was a step ahead of her and she couldn't get to him in time. The premonition hit with such force, her knees buckled. She doubled over and fell to the ground.

And then she was drowning. And screaming. *Help! Help!* But no one could hear her. She had no voice.

I can't breathe! I can't . . .

Flailing, kicking, clawing her way out . . . someone had to help her! She was being sucked under too fast. Something was closing in on her. Water? It was cold, wet, coarse — and it filled her mouth, suffocating her with grainy mouthfuls . . . of sand? She tried to spit it out, shake it off. Climb out, put one hand over the next. *Pull yourself up*, was all she could think. But there was nothing to grab onto. She had no footing. She was going down. Pulled down. To her grave.

No! No! I'm not ready to die — help! Somebody help! Alex . . . !

She was ready to give in, couldn't fight anymore. Then a pair of giant hands grasped her rib cage and pulled her up and out.

"You're okay! You're okay!" She heard Shane, but he was far away, alarmed. "Come out of it, Cam! That's it, open your eyes —"

She was on the ground, on the moss-covered cobblestones. Hyperventilating. Her head was pounding, and Shane was kneeling beside her, scanning her eyes.

Shaking, sweating, Cam clutched his arms.

"What happened?" he asked. "Are you sick?"

"I had . . ." Something stopped Cam from finishing the sentence. He hadn't recognized what was happening to her. Maybe that was as it should be — and stay. Info best kept to herself. For now. "I got dizzy," she said.

"You're still shaking," he noted. "Sure you're all right?"

She was, but for how long? There hadn't been a single time in all her life that her premonitions hadn't come true. This had been her first of her own death.

She wanted Alex. She needed her sister. Now.

"Come on," Shane was saying gently as he helped her to her feet. "Let's go to the Village Plaza. I'll get you some herbal tea. If you don't feel better, I'll bring you back home."

She almost protested. She almost said, No, I'll go

back now. If she couldn't be with Alex, she wanted to be with Miranda. Maybe she should tell her mother about these last two visions — and last night's discovery. But Shane was urging her forward, smiling at her, telling her he'd be there to catch her if she got dizzy again.

And though she'd vowed to be cautious this time, she believed him.

The Village Plaza was the center of town, usually bustling with witches and warlocks of all generations. Ringed by dozens of inviting shops, open-air markets, and cafés with outdoor tables shaded by big, colorful umbrellas, it reminded Cam of a peaceful artists' colony — one that hadn't yet been cheesed up with chain stores and T-shirt souvenirs. Triangular flags and window boxes overflowing with flowers upped the fairy-tale feel of the place.

"Let's go get that tea." Shane led her to a café called the Rive Gauche. "And maybe something sweet to go with it. Could I talk you into that?"

Okay, so maybe it was coincidence, but Cam thought . . . *not*.

The Rive Gauche Café had only one group of customers clustered around a large outdoor table. There were five of them about Cam's age, and one was awfully familiar. Accent on *awful*.

And sarcastic. "To what do we owe a visit by the

DuBaer heiress? The princess of power . . . she who could kill with her eyes but would do no harm and spare even her enemies?"

Sersee. The vicious witch who had been so cruel, so hurtful, so bent on destroying Cam and Alex. Her haughty highness tossed her head, dramatically casting off her hood to free a cascade of ebony curls. She caught Cam in the crosshairs of her piercing violet eyes.

Cam stared back hard. The scary vision of a little while ago? Over it. She shot back, "To what do we owe the opening remarks, insincere though they be?"

The revelation that the leader of the Furies had been twice abandoned — once by parents killed in a fire, then by a Protector who had failed her — tempered Cam's righteous anger. Not that she felt sorry for the Serster, but the burning desire to clobber her had dissolved. Instead, Cam was peeved at Shane — clearly he'd spread the word of her visit.

"Welcome." Sersee's expression was anything but. "Come join us at the Coventry equivalent of the popular table at the lunchroom. We wanted to make you feel right at home. No Starbucks, no sushi, no slice of Beverly Hills pizza, but we can do tasty tea, hot chocolate, and ice cream with the best. And our herbal remedies are . . . to die for."

How convenient, Cam noted, there were two empty seats.

Shane said, "It's up to you, Cam. Want to go someplace else?"

Well, *duh,* she thought.

"Oh, not yet!" Sersee exclaimed. "We must introduce Lady DuBaer to her future subjects."

Shane scowled. "Enough, Sersee."

She ignored him. "Of course there's Epie —" The intro was unnecessary. Cam recognized the grinning moon-faced girl. She was Sersee's most loyal lapdog. "She's kind of hard to miss," the violet-eyed witch added.

Hard to miss? Was the queen of mean dissing her faithful stooge? Epie was chubby but not grotesque — except in the friends she chose. The plump girl tried to laugh now but her face had turned crimson. "At least let me say sorry about what happened last time." She continued gamely, "You remember me, right?"

How could Cam forget? Epie was the most clueless of the Furies. As trusting and devoted to Sersee as their third partner, Michaelina, was wily and cunning. The three had been formidable enemies. "We got punished for what we did," Epie informed her, as if that now made it all right, the slate wiped clean.

She's cute, man! One of the warlocks, a kid with

long dark brown hair and full lips, was giving her silent props. He introduced himself as Rowan. His friend, a boy with a long face and sour expression, was Serle.

That left one other young witch, a gray-eyed girl with straight chin-length dark hair, who was not just looking at Cam but intently studying her. Where had Cam seen her before?

The girl grinned suddenly. "I'm Amaryllis. I work at Crailmore. I've seen you there. Rowan's right. You're very pretty."

Cam smiled, flattered despite her suspicions that the girl and the rest of the crew were Sersee's new slaves, faithful, fresh recruits to the Furies. It crossed her mind that Amaryllis, since she worked at Thantos's fortress, might have a dual allegiance — to Sersee and also to Cam's treacherous uncle. Was she here to spy on Cam?

"I'm not a slave, you know," Amaryllis bristled, answering Cam's unasked question. "Lord Thantos pays us well, and allows liberal time off."

"What a guy," Cam deadpanned.

Shane settled into one of the empty chairs, assuming they were staying. Before Cam could join him, Sersee unexpectedly seized her arm. "I need to speak with her in private," she announced to the gathering. "I'm sure no one minds."

"I do." Cam tore her arm away, but Sersee's quick hand grasped her waist and swept her along, whispering, "Please. What I have to say is not for public knowledge.

"They all look up to me," she added when they were behind the café, "and I want to keep it that way. Anyway, I regret any inconvenience I might've caused you in the past."

Inconvenience? That was like the doctor saying you may feel some "discomfort" before plunging you into horrible, stinging, unbearable pain. Exactly what Sersee had caused her.

"I am sorry," Sersee reiterated. "I want to make it up to you."

Cam brushed her off. "Take a memo, Betty Spaghetty. Sorry doesn't begin to do it."

The violet-eyed witch continued as if she were reading off a TelePrompTer. "You stole Shane from me. I hurt you because I was jealous."

"Hurt me? You turned me into a hamster! You tried to kill me!" Cam heard herself squeaking like one, as she shuddered at the memory.

As if envy made attempted murder forgivable, Sersee continued, "Shane was so *obvious* about it. I was betrayed. I gave him a place to stay, helped him when he was down and out. And then you come along and he kicks me to the curb. Me! Treats me like some big, fat, bad nobody."

Cam was beyond unconvinced. "That's awful, Sersee. He should have treated you like the skinny, sneaky, nobody you really are."

To her credit, the Serster didn't take the bait. She changed tactics, played the pity card. "I was enraged. You had it all — a home, a family, money, admiration because of who you are, not for anything you accomplished. I had nothing. No parents, not even a Protector who wanted me. Then you invade my turf and steal my boyfriend."

"Your turf? I must have missed the sign that said 'Serseeville: Enter at your own risk.' I came to honor Lord Karsh" — Cam could feel herself choking up — "to attend his funeral. I didn't know Shane was your boyfriend. I thought . . ." she trailed off and shrugged.

Sersee's stab at remorse was lame. "I acted rashly and hatefully. I used my powers to hurt, not to heal. If I were you, I would never forgive me. But" — she looked up hopefully — "I'm not you. You're a better person than I could ever be."

The devious witch was using her own meanness as a defense? No wonder she was first among Furies. Cam gave her major kudos for shamelessness.

"Anyway." Sersee took Cam's arm again and walked around the side of the café, where the others were. She whispered confidentially, "See Rowan over there? He's my new —"

"— quarry?" Cam suggested.

"Lucky boy." Sersee didn't miss a beat. "So Shane is all yours."

"Thanks for your leftovers."

"Leftovers? I don't think so." Sersee's violet eyes betrayed a flicker of anger. "Shane A. Wright is the most coveted young warlock on the island, a real 'catch' as you mainlanders might say. Any witch would give her best crystal stone for a chance with him. He's brilliant, ambitious, easy on the eyes, *and* from one of Coventry's most important families."

That was news to Cam. All Shane had said about his parents was they'd kicked him out.

"I have an idea," Sersee was saying. "Tomorrow I'll show you around the island. It'll be just us girls. I can show you where were the best stuff is —"

"Speaking of just us girls, bad things come in threes," Cam interrupted. "Where's the caboose of your cabal — Michaelina?"

"Mike's still in lockdown. For her part in, well, the thing that happened with you and Alex."

"Lockdown?"

Sersee laughed. "She's still serving her sentence; doing community service."

Baap! Red flag. Scrappy Michaelina was still doing penance while slithery Sersee and her slavishly loyal fan Epie were already free? Did not track.

"So now that the air is clear and you've forgiven me," Sersee continued as if just saying it made it true, "hang with us for a while. We were just about to leave for our Summer Solstice ceremony. Okay, we're a little behind — the real holiday was last month. But it's fun. You might like it. Of course, you're not really a full witch yet. So if you're afraid . . ." She let it trail provocatively.

Grabbing Shane and splitting, Cam thought, was probably the real fun thing to do. But — even though she knew Sersee was playing her — she wouldn't have minded checking out the witchy ritual.

Also on the "go with" side: the chance to observe Coventry's "best catch" in his natural habitat. As long as that didn't include any place she could drown.

"Is that true?" Shane asked, bringing her a steaming cup of fragrant tea. "You're up for the Summer Solstice ceremony?"

"It could be interesting," Cam conceded.

"Oh, totally," Epie squealed, then cast a quick glance at Sersee to see if she'd said the right thing.

Oh, she had, all right. In a way Cam could never have counted on.

CHAPTER EIGHT
YOU WANT FRIES WITH THAT?

Alex had almost forgotten.

Back home in Montana, she'd always worked — after school, weekends, vacations, and every summer. So had her friends. Her mom, Sara, had worked *three* jobs to make ends meet.

No matter how much the actual jobs reeked, for Alex, being able to contribute to the household, help Sara make ends meet, and be able to buy her own stuff — whether it was a new CD, a movie ticket, or a thrift shop splurge — had felt right and real. It was that feeling she'd almost forgotten.

"Just because you live in cutesyville with the

Barneses," Michaelina had chided her, "you had to become one of them?"

Okay, so it had taken a sneaky little sorceress to pound the point home. Color her reminded. Independence? Alex was all over it.

She knew exactly where to start. College-bound Jason had worked at Marble Bay's premier pizza joint, Pie in the Sky. Had they replaced him yet?

Alex got Michaelina to change into civilian clothes, and they hopped a bus into town. They were outside the pizza place, peeking in the window, when suddenly a woman came flying out the door looking grim and in a hurry. Alex recognized her as PITS's cranky waitress, Irene Palmer.

"Hi —" Alex started, but was drowned out by Mr. Tagliere, the manager, who'd followed Irene, yelling, "You can't do that! You can't quit without giving me notice! It's against the law!"

Without turning, Irene responded with a spiteful, "Buh-bye," and a flutter of her bloodred fingertips. She brushed by the girls so quickly Alex had to duck not to be nailed by her huge shoulder bag.

PITS was now two wait-staff short. Alex and Mike were hired on the spot — no questions asked, except, "Can you start today?"

"How cool is this?" Juiced, Alex smoothed down her cheesy red-and-white-striped PITS apron. "I knew there'd be one opening, but two? And she quit just as we got there. I can't believe our lu —" She trailed off and rounded on Michaelina. "You didn't. Tell me you didn't."

Michaelina was writing out her name tag. She shrugged innocently. "Well, how fun would it be without you? That was the whole point of coming here."

"We're supposed to help people, not swell the Massachusetts unemployment rolls." Alex got in her face. "What did you do? And how soon can you undo it?"

"Get over it." Mike grinned. "Irene is gone. She was already thinking she was too hot to sling hash. Didn't you catch her attitude? I read it through the window. All I did was agree with her. I sent her a message suggesting she was wasting her time in a paltry pizza place when she could do so much better."

Alex began to untie her apron. The plan? Ball it up, fling it at Michaelina, and split. But there was Mr. Tagliere looking so happy and relieved, and here she was, about to do what she'd sworn she would do when she first got to Marble Bay. She was going to pay her own way. She was on the way back to being the person she'd once been.

Except, back then, there hadn't been Cade. And it

suddenly occurred to her — as Mr. Tag put a tray of steaming pizza in her hands — that she would probably be working PITS's busiest shifts — evenings and weekends.

She glanced at Michaelina, who was already at a corner booth busily sponging down a table. Had the mischievous imp realized what Alex hadn't? That this job would severely cut into prime Cade time.

Mr. Tagliere called a quick conference right after Alex delivered her first tray. He gave them the download on the salary-plus-tips system, how to place orders, how to treat patrons.

He hadn't thought to mention rules like "no mind reading, no food levitating, no magick when dealing with disruptive customers." Which was, considering Michaelina's penchant for trouble, a serious omission.

Her first customers were sisters, about thirteen and nine years old. They'd barely slid into the booth when Mike advised the younger one, "I wouldn't go with the extra cheese, it'll get stuck in those wires on your teeth." The child's hand flew to her braces-filled mouth and her eyes went wide.

To the stunned older girl, the wild little witch urged, "Forget the diet pizza. Matt won't like you better if you lose weight. Go ahead, pig out on the sausage, peppers, and mushrooms."

What are you doing? Are you crazy? Fearful of having her own witchness blown, Alex was flabbergasted. But the sisters hadn't stalked out. They took Mike's advice instead.

What? Michaelina innocently demanded of Alex. *I'm helping people. That's my job.*

Alex gritted her teeth. *Wrong. Your job is to bring them what they order, without commentary!*

The put-upon pixie shrugged and rolled her eyes.

"Hey, I didn't order yet," shouted a portly man as Michaelina headed to the kitchen.

She whirled and shot him a smile. "Sure you did. It was between the chicken parm and the sausage hero. You went with the chicken. I have it right here. . . ." She showed him her order pad.

Michaelina soon found other ways to "help." She added selective herbs to the orders, "for better digestion." She sprinkled soothing nettle on the pasta of a patron who'd complained of stomach pains, and mallow on the sausage-and-pepper sub of a woman with an eye infection. She added a healthy pinch of wormwood to the salad of a kid she deemed too thin. "Wormwood stimulates the appetite," she told Alex in passing. "This is a good deed."

The moment Alex allowed herself to believe the little witch, things changed.

While most people didn't notice Michaelina's potent pizza potions, the regulars did. One disgruntled customer sent his spaghetti and meatballs back, bellowing that it tasted like turpentine.

"Don't blame the waitress," his wife chastised him.

Oh, yes, definitely blame the waitress, Alex thought, shaking her head at Mike, who stood her ground. *It was thyme, not turpentine. The guy needed a mouthwash! Pee-eew! I mean, what would* you *have done?*

The wayward elf was beyond stoked. And soon her glee turned contagious.

Alex gave up spying on and scolding Mike. She herself had used magick in the past to get even with kids who gave her a hard time. Of course, back then she hadn't really known what she was doing and her powers hadn't been as impressive as they were now.

Alex spent her entire break on the phone with Cade, who was surprised — Alex hadn't told him she was job hunting — but supportive. "I get it, I really do," he assured her. "It feels good to accomplish something on your own. And if working helps you get back to who you were, well, I want to know that girl, too. I want to know everything about you."

She melted. She'd been right. Cade was a keeper.

"What does Cam say about your new career direction? Will she want in on the action when she gets back?" Cade teased.

Cam! Alex hadn't told her, hadn't communicated with her twin in days. How weird was that? The closest she'd come was "e-personating" Cam, finally sending that e-mail to the cruising Dave and Emily.

The action at PITS really picked up during the evening shift.

A group of middle-school kids came in, three boys and two girls whose idea of a good time consisted of flinging spaghetti, dousing one another with their soft drinks, and pouring sugar all over the table.

Mike and Alex looked at each other and, with barely visible grins, were on it so fast, the kids didn't know what hit them. As they lifted their forks to sling pasta across the booth, their spaghetti boomeranged back, snaked up their noses, matted their hair, splashed rivers of sauce into their ears. When the tossed drinks froze in midair and the sugar coiled back into the dispenser, they jumped back, awestruck and speechless. Alex made sure they settled the check before bolting.

Later, a couple of big-attitude biker boys came in looking for trouble. But targeting Michaelina? So unfortunate.

The one with the shiny slicked-back hair leered at the little witch. "Hey, small fry —" He winked to his partner before turning back to Mike. "Get me a small order of fries. Get it?"

His pal tried to top him. "Yo, that's not her name. Check the name tag, it's Thumbelina."

Michaelina gave them a thumbs-up — and a pitying gaze before going to fetch their pie. Their next clever words were "mmmrrrph" and "grrumrruurph," as oddly sticky pizza cheese superglued their mouths shut.

"What'd you say? Speak up!" Mike dared them as, red-faced and sweating, they pointed to their mouths and pounded on the table. That brought the attention of nearby customers, who found the sight of two mute thugs a total hoot.

Michaelina ended the torment after a minute or so, advising them sagely, "See what happens when you're rude? It's instant karma, dudes."

Throwing a pair of twenty-dollar bills at her, they bailed.

Then she went too far. A stuck-up blond came in, totally putting down the girl who'd come with her. "Who cut your hair? Edward Scissorhands? It looks awful."

Mike, the avenging elf, arrived at their table carrying a steaming pie. Somehow the piping-hot cheese — all of it — slid off the dough, heading for the diss queen's lap. Alex was aghast. Nasty as she was, Snob Girl was wearing shorts and was about to be badly burned. Alex moved without thinking, stopped the cheese in midair, and slid it back onto the tray, glaring at Michaelina.

She deserves it! Mike insisted. Again the sizzling mozzarella slipped off the pie. This time Alex caught it in her hand and yelped as the hot cheese seared her palm.

Mike gasped and jumped back as if expecting Alex to hit her. When it didn't happen, she quickly and gratefully took the twice-reconstituted pie and Alex back to the kitchen. Streaming apologies, she reached into her herb pouch and found cooling, curing herbs to rub on the wound.

"Enough," Alex declared.

By closing time, they were both exhausted. Since Alex had Casa Barnes to herself, she invited Michaelina to stay over. While they waited for Cade outside PITS, Michaelina sat on the curb and counted her tips. Her eyes twinkled. "Who knew the mainland was so fun? And so profitable!" She stashed the take in her pocket, while Alex watched the road for the McDonalds' SUV, which Cade was borrowing to take them home.

"Cade, Cade, Cade." Michaelina stretched her legs and leaned back, palms against the sidewalk. "Is he that . . . special? Is he, like, the One?"

"Could be," Alex answered. "I keep thinking how my mom — Sara, my adoptive mom, my protector — would have liked him."

"Yeah, but she's dead. Hey, wait a minute —" Mike snapped her fingers as if she'd just had a brilliant idea.

"Why don't we ask her? We could, you know, bring her . . . not her exactly, but her spirit back. For a little while."

"You're kidding, right?" Even as she said it, Alex realized that it could be done. Why had she never thought of it before? Hadn't she and Cam, albeit accidentally, called up the spirit of their grandmother Leila DuBaer? Why not summon Sara?

She couldn't speak, wasn't even sure she was still breathing. She'd be sixteen soon, the age of Initiation. She'd be a full-fledged witch then. Would Sara be proud of her?

And what would her mom really have thought about Cade?

And what of the girl she was becoming, this long year spent without each other? What would Sara Fielding think of Alex now?

It had been so long since she'd had anyone, anyone who'd known and loved her all her life, to talk to. She longed to see Sara again, to tell her everything and find out what she thought. And what advice she'd offer —

Alex looked hard at Michaelina. The petite sorceress was telling her she could find out.

CHAPTER NINE
SUMMER SOLSTICE

The Summer Solstice celebration took place in the woods at sunset. The participants, Sersee, Epie, Amaryllis, Rowan, and Serle, brought satchels containing herbs, stones, candles in jars, cookies — and one raw egg.

Epie excitedly started to explain what each ingredient was for, but Sersee clapped a hand over the naive girl's mouth. "You'll find out soon enough," she told Cam. "Don't you want to be surprised?"

By Sersee? Not, Cam thought.

Shane squeezed her hand and whispered, "The ceremony's easy. Nothing to worry about."

Cam fell in with the group as they trekked deeper into the woods. She could hang with them as long as she didn't get lulled into feeling like one of them. Trust was something they'd have to earn.

The forests of Coventry were spectacular, she thought, enjoying the crunching sound of pine needles underfoot, the fresh, clean smells, and the vibrant colors. The first line of a poem came to her —

The woods are lovely, dark and deep . . .

What was the next line? She couldn't remember.

They reached a grove of purple alder trees. Nature had given them bright berries and saw-toothed leaves. Sersee's decorating committee had decked them out in silver and white ribbons. Beyond the festive grove was their destination, a small, circular pond.

Water. Her premonition.

Cam flinched, started to back away.

"What's wrong?" Shane asked.

"I . . . c-can't," she stammered. "I mean, I wasn't expecting water."

"The pond's just an element in the ceremony," Shane told her. "It's the shape of it, nature's perfect circle. No one goes in."

But wasn't that the point of the circle, to be inside it? Cam wondered. Shane offered to take her back if she felt uncomfortable, but in the end, she opted to stay and observe the ceremony.

Each person took a place around the pond. Sitting

cross-legged, they each placed a stone of quartz crystal to their right and another of gold to the left. "Quartz opens us to psychic powers," Shane explained. "And the gold is to attract abundance and riches in the coming year."

The tea candles were set down next, ringing the pond. Sersee rose to her knees and passed around one tapered candle to light all the others.

Then, as if passing a verbal baton, each person took a turn explaining the meaning of the ceremony. It was about the anticipation of plenty, the bounty of nature, hopes for the coming harvest. As advertised, it was simple but impressive and benevolent. It reminded Cam of the Coventry credo, the words etched on the Unity Dome, "that all things might grow to their most bountiful goodness."

In time, she relaxed, even joined in as they stood, held hands, and skipped around the pond. One by one, each jumped over the candles — whoever jumped highest, it was said, would have the most success in the coming year. Because of Cam's natural athleticism and soccer training, she was easily the highest jumper.

Shane jubilantly raised her arm in celebration. Sersee brought the mood down. "If we're finished worshiping heiress DuBaer, we're ready for the next part," she sullenly announced.

Bring it on, Cam thought, beginning to enjoy this.

Sersee clapped her hands, and Epie opened the satchel containing the cookies. "We close our eyes and take —"

"One cookie each — emphasis on *one,* Epie," Sersee reminded the girl.

The chunky witch reddened again. "Um, they're all the same," she told Cam, trying to ignore her leader. "They're all the same except for the burned one."

"And believe me," Sersee taunted her disciple again, "Epie would even gobble down the burned one if we didn't keep an eye on her."

"Cut it out!" Epie said with surprising spunk.

Cam looked from one of them to the other. Sersee had always treated Epie more like an unloved pet than a person. But Epie had never even tried to defend herself. Her effort now — weak and ineffectual as it was — surprised Cam. She felt almost affectionate toward the girl. But just because Epie was becoming "her enemy's enemy," Cam reminded herself, didn't make her Cam's friend.

"Go on," Sersee ordered her. "Finish explaining."

"The person who picks the burned cookie," Epie continued, glowering at Sersee, as if daring her to interrupt again, "has to leap over the candles three times while the person who baked the cookies throws the egg, trying to . . . um, hit that person . . . and then we all —"

"Enough." The raven-haired witch silenced her. "You're making it too complicated."

Serle stepped in front of the brooding Epie. "It's very simple," he explained. "If the egg misses, the person jumping will have great fortune in the coming year. If it hits, each of us has to give a small gift to the jumper, to lend him or her the luck they're lacking."

Everyone who thinks, Huh? raise their hand, Cam thought. Only Shane laughed. The satchel was passed around. Predictably, Cam got the last cookie — the burned one.

"Don't you seem to be the special one today?" Sersee remarked. "Let's see how well you do with Amaryllis aiming for you — she's the one who baked them."

Cam was up for the challenge. Her innate competitiveness — combined with disgust at the shabby way Sersee had been treating Epie — fueled her desire to ace this game and show Sersee up.

She brushed off her shorts and skipped around the candles, once, twice . . . still, Amaryllis had not pitched the egg. Cam was almost finished with the third go-round when she saw it hurtling toward her.

She was trying to duck out of the way when a sudden powerful blast of air hit her, striking her solar plexus like an icy fist. In the split second before she tumbled backward, she caught sight of Epie. The girl's cheeks were puffed out and her mouth was puckered as if it were she, and not nature, who'd blown Cam over.

A split second of eye contact followed by Epie's apologetic shrug told Cam that, improbable as it was, Sersee's punching bag had provided the gust that sent Cam plummeting into the pond.

Immediately, she felt a tidal pull in the murky water, a whirling force dragging her down. Her feet found the pond's floor, which, instead of stopping her descent, seemed to open beneath her, sucking her down farther. There was no bottom. There was only sand. Quicksand.

Cam knew that flailing would only drag her deeper; she knew that crying out could fill her mouth and then her lungs with water and thick suffocating grit. She struggled against the desire to yell, to wrestle up and out of the soft, squashy sand. Her terrifying premonition was coming true.

No! her brain screamed. *No, this can't be happening!* But her visions always meant something. Why hadn't she listened to the warning?

She swung her arms around, her hands grasping for something, anything firm enough to pull herself back up. Nothing held.

She could feel the gritty dirt rising around her; she could already taste the coarse, granular mud. She could resist no more. "Help! Help!" she screamed as the sand rose around her. Why hadn't anyone rushed in to save her?

She could see Shane on his knees at the perimeter of the pond. "Hang on!" he was calling. "I'm coming!" But all he was doing was stretching out his arm, reaching out for her. And he wasn't close enough.

Cam put one hand over the next and went into coaching mode. *Pull yourself up. You can do it. Don't panic. Concentrate!* She was up to her neck in quicksand now. She bent her knee, trying to push off, to force a dent in the thick sludge, anything temporarily sturdy enough. But every time she lifted her knee, the sand collapsed around her.

She was sinking fast, the thick swampy water bubbling around her neck. Desperately, she reached for her sun charm. Would its strange power help her? By what magick could she forge a way out of this? She didn't know —

The sand reached her chin. It felt as if she were wearing a bodysuit of mud filled with scratching, scrabbling insects. And all she could do was flail her arms, pull, push, stretch, claw. *Just keep moving,* she told herself, *someone will reach you*. The pond wasn't that wide. And they were witches! Surely they could find a long branch, something sturdy she could hang on to.

Unless, of course . . .

The last thought unglued her completely. It had been a trap after all.

Out of nowhere, the last line of the poem about the woods came to her. . . . *But I have promises to keep, and miles to go before I sleep.* The long sleep of death, that's what it was about. The poet was saying it wasn't his time to die. And it wasn't hers, either!

She screamed, "Get a branch! Hurry!" But as she threw back her head to breathe, sand filled her ears and she could not hear.

Cam fought to breathe, to keep her head above water until someone came. Miranda! Wouldn't her mother know? Couldn't she sense Cam's peril? Surely someone who loved her was on the way. *Alex!* her frantic racing mind screamed as the watery sand slipped into her mouth. She tried to expel it, spit it out. It was no use. She was sinking, being swallowed alive. *Alex . . .*

CHAPTER TEN
A CRY FOR HELP

Help! Help! I'm drowning!

Alex woke with a start, bathed in sweat. She was hyperventilating, so dizzy she almost passed out when she tried to sit up. The nightmare that had jolted her awake was gale force. It felt so real. . . .

I'm going down! It's taking me . . . I can't pull myself out . . . Alex!

Alex blinked, tried to shake the blanket of sleep off her, to think clearly. She'd fallen asleep early, the minute she'd come home from her full first day of work, and still wasn't fully awake. She checked the clock; it wasn't even midnight. She must've fallen into some deep pit of a nightmare.

Alex! Alex, where are you? I'm drowning!

It was Cam! Her sister had been summoning her. But wasn't Cam —? Alex looked over at her sister's side of the room. Her bed was emp —

She remembered. Cam was on Coventry Island. Had left just days ago.

Please help me! I don't want to die!

Snap! Alex's eyes suddenly opened wide. This was a nightmare, all right, the nastiest kind. Because it was real. Worse, this was not something about to happen — this terrified cry was real and now. Cam was sending her a telepathic 911.

Alex leaped out of bed, tried to calm herself just enough to think straight. Miranda! Ileana! They were on Coventry. Couldn't they rescue Cam? She ran for the phone. And stopped dead.

There was no number to call. Coventry Island had no phones.

She refocused swiftly and went the telepathic route, calling out desperately, *Miranda! Ileana! Cam's in trouble. Hurry! You've got to save her!*

She waited. Listening hard. All she heard were the sounds of the Marble Bay summer night, the clicking of cicadas, the barking of a nearby dog, the whirr of the air conditioner. No return message from Miranda or Ileana. And then —

It's pulling me down! I can't get out! Someone save me!

The panic now seized Alex's entire body, propelled her forward. She flew downstairs to the kitchen, as if the answer might lie there. Her eyes fell on the spice rack. The Transporter spell! That was it! She could use magick to transfer herself to Coventry and save Cam. She was shaking hard, trying to hold the small spice bottles still to decipher the labels, trying to remember which she needed. One that started with M — but what? Margarine? No! No, stupid, marjoram . . . or did that bring back the dead?

In her panic, Alex stopped thinking altogether. She opened every spice jar and matched it up with any and every incantation that came to her.

Hold on, Cam! I'm coming! It'll be okay! I just have to get the spell —

The door banged open. Alex jumped.

A blur of green rushed at her.

Michaelina shouted, "What's wrong? I heard you calling out —"

"It's Cam!" Alex yelled. "She's . . . I heard her . . ."

She trailed off. So, wait. Alex's telepathic messages to Coventry had been intercepted by . . . Michaelina?

There was no time for questions. A crystal! That's what she needed! The one Karsh had given her was in the bedroom. She raced toward the stairs.

Michaelina yelled after her, "I'll help you. Don't worry. I have an idea."

"We have no time —" Alex screamed back at her.

"I have a spell I can do," Mike promised, rushing to catch up with her. "We can see her. See what's happening. And I can pull her out of — I mean, we can save her."

"I think she's drowning!" Alex was trembling now, terrified that she'd wasted too much time, that her sister was already —

"Then let's move it!" Mike shouted. She blasted up the steps, beating Alex into the bedroom.

Alex's heart was racing. What if they saw the trouble Cam was in and they couldn't help her? Would that be worse? And could Michaelina even do this? Once Thantos had located the missing Dylan, by using a powerful spell called the Situator. But the head of the DuBaer dynasty was an experienced tracker, practiced in magick, extraordinarily skilled. The childlike witch in front of Alex was none of the above. But Alex could not afford to doubt her.

Michaelina seized a glass jar from Cam's desk and flipped back its mirrored, spring-loaded lid. Inside was a vanilla-bean candle. "Light it!" she commanded.

With what? Alex looked frantically around the room. Cam could have ignited the wick with her blazing eyes. Alex had no such ability, and no match. Her talent was telekinesis. She shut her eyes and focused all her fear and desperation on one image: a flame. The fire she'd pictured hadn't even turned red, when a drawer opened and a book of matches leaped out, landing in her hands.

From a leather pouch inside her cape pocket, Michaelina withdrew a rose quartz crystal, which she placed beside the candle, and a small familiar-looking brownish root. When she tossed it into the candle flame, Alex caught a faint aroma of apple. "This is mandrake root," the intense little witch announced. "Sometimes called witch's apple. I'm going to add a pinch of henbane, then keep your eyes on the fire light. We should see Cam in a minute."

"And we'll be able to help her . . . save her, right?" Alex insisted.

Michaelina didn't answer.

CHAPTER ELEVEN
THE RESCUE

Cam's life flashed before her in movie-style slo-mo. She was kicking, her chubby legs were like scissors as David Barnes hoisted baby Cam in the air.

She was snuggled in Emily's lap, listening raptly to *Goodnight Moon*.

She was the proud big sister rocking baby Dylan.

She was running through the house in Marble Bay, riding her two-wheeler to school, jumping on the bed during a sleepover at Beth's house, booting her first soccer goal . . .

And then she was in Montana, looking into Alex's eyes for the first time, feeling complete. Whole. Saved.

Something huge, hard as steel tongs, seized her rib

cage. Hands, she realized, feeling a pulse pushing through the palms of whatever mammoth creature was gripping her waist and pulling her up through the dark ooze. An angry voice echoed, as if through a megaphone, "What have you done?!"

The viselike grip held firm. Cam was being ripped out of the warmth, out of the deadly clinging slime, out of the murky water. Before she could completely process what was going on, she was being wrapped in a heavy blanket and set down gently on the ground. Then the sound of her own coughing drowned out everything else. She sensed someone massaging her back. These hands were softer, lighter than the ones that had dragged her out of the pond. She knew it was Shane. He was shaking, calling to her, "It's all right, you're safe. . . ."

She understood. She'd been brought back, saved. But not by him.

The recognition of who had rescued her dawned slowly and made her sick to her already twisting stomach: Thantos DuBaer. Her detested uncle had materialized out of nowhere and had done what no one else could or wanted to — rushed into the deadly pond, reached down, and plucked her out. Pulled her from darkness to light. Saved her life.

"I demand an explanation!" Cam heard him bellowing at the group. "How could you let this happen to my niece?"

Their answers, coming in a jumble all at once, betrayed their trembling fear. Cam heard fragments. "Summer Solstice . . . the candles . . . an accident . . ."

"An accident?" Thantos roared. "Not one of you brilliant witches or highly trained warlocks could rescue her?"

"We tried, my lord. . . ." Shane sounded lame, even to Cam's clogged ears.

"If I find this to be a prank of some kind, punishment will be swift. And severe," her uncle continued coldly. "Now get out, all of you!"

Cam was still coughing, shivering, her teeth would not stop chattering. Shane was holding her, but Thantos tore him away. "Maggot! First you betrayed me, now you betray my niece?! You who would be a hero! How dare you allow this to happen to her? Get out of my sight! At once!"

It was Thantos's massive black cape she'd been wrapped in. It held his bitter aura, the scent of the predator. Cam knew she ought to have been flooded with relief, gratitude. Instead, she wondered if his rage at Shane was fueled by the anger of not killing her himself.

"You cannot possibly believe that," the outraged tracker barked. Kneeling beside her now, he had easily read her mind.

"I don't know what to believe," she said out loud.

The hulking warlock stood abruptly and pulled her to her feet. From behind a grove of dark evergreens, Cam heard a horse whinny. Thantos snapped his fingers and Epona, or his twin, trotted out of the shadows. Before she could protest, Thantos had lifted Cam again — this time depositing her onto the enormous horse's broad back. "We'll get you back to Crailmore," he told her as she desperately seized the saddle horn. "Miranda will take care of you. . . ."

He stared expectantly at Cam. With effort, she held his challenging gaze and nervously said, "Thank you."

Thantos laid a hand on the great horse's shiny neck, steadying the beast. "Then you can repay me —"

Cam stared at him. "What?"

Her uncle's bellowing laugh caused the high-strung animal to paw the ground. "I demand nothing but your attention. I have things to tell you. And you must listen without prejudice. Not too high a price to pay, in exchange for your life, wouldn't you agree?"

Before she could answer, he smacked the stallion's flanks and sent him galloping toward the cliffs of Crailmore.

CHAPTER TWELVE
"I COULDN'T SAVE YOU"

The flame danced, and a picture of Cam appeared inside the mirrored lid of the candle jar. She was submerged in water. But she was all right. Lolling against the porcelain ledge of a bathtub, Cam's auburn hair was slicked back, dripping wet, her gray eyes were closed, soapy water reached to her shoulders, and she was breathing normally.

Alex's racing heart slowed at the sight. The prickly tension left her body in a *whoosh* of relief and she collapsed on the floor, barely aware of Michaelina's self-congratulatory told-you-so babble.

The sprightly sorceress had done it, pulled off the Situator spell. Even as Alex began to relax, she knew that something bad *had* happened to her sister and that the SOS she'd received was real. But Cam's pose was classic; her twin was in post-trauma mode. Whatever the threat had been, she was all right now. Alex had no strength left to find out exactly what had happened. She'd catch her breath, she decided, then connect later. She lay on the floor, staring at the ceiling.

"So, what, you're going to fall asleep on me?" Michaelina mischievously demanded. "Before you even thank me?"

"Pretty much," Alex murmured. She yawned and closed her eyes.

Someone was poking her. The first thing Alex saw when she opened her eyes was the last thing she'd seen before closing them. Michaelina.

The wiry witch was sitting cross-legged on the floor next to Alex, cheek resting in her palm. "Do you always sleep this late?"

"Only when I've been wrenched awake by a twin in mortal danger. What time is it, anyway?"

"Four —"

What? Alex bolted upright. She'd slept all day — missed work, missed Cade?

"In the morning," Mike informed her.

Alex fell back down. "Tell me this is your idea of a

joke." She turned on her side, her back to Michaelina. "And then tell me — not to be rude — but 'see ya later' would work. Tell me you're leaving now."

"I *am* leaving. So are you. Assuming you still want to do what we talked about yesterday?"

They'd said a lot of things —

"Sara," the pixie reminded Alex. "If we go now, we can get to the sacred ground before dawn. That's the best time to call up the spirits of the dead." Michaelina rushed to the phone and began dialing. "We'll have to get to Salem before sunrise," she announced. "So I'm calling us a cab. No use wasting time and energy on traveling spells. We'll need all we can muster to work out a visit with your lost protector."

Suddenly, Alex wasn't sure. It was true that she longed to see Sara again, Sara, the best and only mother she'd known for fourteen of her fifteen years. But right now? Like this? With Michaelina in charge?

"I resent that." Having ordered a taxi, the wounded witch slammed down the receiver. "Didn't I help you see that your Wonder twin was safe and sound? Look around. Aren't I the only one in this room who knows the right herbs, crystals, incantations? Unless you'd like to wing it —"

How do *you* know such an advanced spell? Alex

found herself thinking. To her knowledge, neither Mike nor the other Furies had ever been initiated.

"Through no fault of our own, I assure you," Michaelina snapped. "But we *have* watched more initiations and snagged more secret books and picked up more tricks of the trade from unwitting Coventry initiates than most so-called *acceptable* fledglings. Trust me, I can get you to your mom faster than Ileana and Miranda combined. Especially since neither of them seems available or inclined to help you or your sister at the moment."

Alex let the sarcasm slide. The pint-sized sorceress sounded very sure of herself. And uncertain as Alex was, she did yearn to hear Sara's rasping voice again, to see her image, even if it was ghostly and not of flesh and blood. It had never really occurred to her to ask her mother, or Ileana, to summon Sara for her.

Once they were in the cab — en route to Salem Woods — the Coventry imp became noticeably edgy.

"Aren't we there yet?" Mike harangued the driver. Snappish and impatient, her certainty that she could pull off the Transporter spell seemed to be fading, giving way to ill-tempered jitters. "You'd better not be taking us out of the way. Hello, do you even know where we're going?"

Why was Mike so jumpy? It wasn't as if Sara's spirit

was waiting in the moonlit grove, tapping her watch and threatening to leave if they were late.

Michaelina immediately picked up Alex's flippant thought. "I'd think you'd take this more seriously," she scolded. "This is your dearly departed mother we're talking about!"

"Speaking of. Why do we have to go all the way to Salem? There are other places where Cam and I have tapped into spirits, like Mariner's Park where —"

"I don't make the rules," Mike retorted. "This is where they said —"

"They? Who's they?" Instantly suspicious, Alex blurted, "This better not be a setup."

"They? Did I say they? And, excuse me, but did you say setup?" Swinging deftly from defensive to insulted, Michaelina drew herself up, though she still barely came up to Alex's shoulder. "You wanted to do this. Are you really getting cold feet about seeing the person who was most important to you? Well, I'm the witch with the power switch. I can make it happen. Unless you don't think I'm capable."

Carefully, Alex said, "Oh, I know you're capable." The question was of what.

Arms folded, Michaelina challenged, "Oh, I get it. You're scared."

She had reason to be. She'd been in the woods of

Salem, Massachusetts, once before. Ghosts roamed the wilderness. Spectral apparitions had come to her as breezes, ruffling her hair, tingling her scalp. She'd smelled musty robes, the charred threads of clothing long ago turned to ash. Something, Cam had hysterically sworn, had reached out and touched her. Alex herself had heard muffled, deep, wounded voices urging her and Cam to go back. Because if they stayed in those woods, the voices warned, he who they loved would follow them and die.

He was Karsh. He had come to save them, just as the spirits had prophesied. And there he had suffered a terrible death.

Alex remembered the stricken old warlock lying on the ground, inside the circle of stones; she could still see Ileana leaning down to comfort him, straining to catch the fallen tracker's last words. Which Alex had heard and, in the grief and fear that had followed his passing, had nearly forgotten. Now she recalled they were about a book. . . .

"Keep the change. Both pennies," Michaelina snapped at the driver, hopping out of the cab and slamming the door. The taxi sped off, leaving her and Alex in a cloud of dust.

To her immense relief, Alex saw that this was not the same area she and Cam had traveled to before. The forest where Lord Karsh had been killed had been near the water, smelling of salt and brine. This place was dry, its ground a bed of soft pine needles.

Still, this woodland was eerie in another way. Alex couldn't put her finger on it until Michaelina led her onto a narrow dirt road that cut through the forest. An old, weather-beaten sign nailed to a tree alongside the path told the story: GALLOWS HILL. This was the executioners' lair. In these very woods, victims of the witch trials not burned or drowned were hanged.

But why would Sara's spirit be here? Sara had been a protector, and though she held firm beliefs about the beauty and bounty of nature and its ability to heal sick souls, she wasn't a witch. And she hadn't been murdered, unless you counted the big C as a killer. Lung cancer, not a noose, had ended Sara's life. Nor had she any ancestors that Alex knew of whose spirits might haunt this place.

"Over there." Michaelina stopped, pointing to a thicket of evergreens. "We'll cast a sacred circle right there."

Alex's stomach lurched. Until this moment, she hadn't completely believed this would happen. Only now it felt very, very real. It sounded real, as if, over the buzz and scramble of forest creatures, someone was breathing, waiting only to be summoned.

Alex sniffed the air, expecting the aroma of violets,

of chamomile and chocolate, her mother's sweet scents. She caught a whiff of something else — medicinal and acrid. . . .

"Pay attention!" Michaelina ordered. With the slim branch in her hand, she scurried to draw a circle in the earth. Even before it was complete, the urchin extracted stones from her drawstring pouch. "Opals to contact the spirit world," she announced. "And lots of marjoram —"

The traveler's herb, Alex knew. Mike's candle was courtesy of the Cami collection, an aromatherapy candle she'd swiped from the nightstand.

"Come inside." Michaelina held out her hand, and Alex took it, stepping into the circle. "Are you ready?"

Numbly, Alex nodded, her pulse pounding in her ears, until she could barely hear the incantation.

In the pale before day, in the dark beyond
    night,
Good spirit, grace us with your light
Grant that Alexandra, the daughter adored,
May see you, and hear you, dear mother,
    once more,
Seeking truth and guidance, she braves this
    black glen.
Be with her now, Sara, as you were with her
    then.

"Don't be upset." Michaelina gave Alex's hand a surprisingly strong squeeze. "She might not look exactly as you remember her."

A breeze picked up and Alex shivered. A faint tinkling gave way to a rustling, to footsteps in the forest. From behind a tangle of trees, a thin, tiny ray of light shone. Alex watched it in awe until its brightness forced her to shut her eyes. When she reopened them, a cloaked figure stood in the shadows, just outside the circle.

Alex's eyes clouded; her throat closed. Was it . . . ?

"Yes, it is. I was hoping you would send for me. I've been waiting."

Alex gasped. Sara's voice — it wasn't . . . hoarse. She spoke in a whisper, but there was no wheezing, no coughing. A wild thought came to Alex. In death, had Sara been cured, the ravages of years of smoking cleansed from her lungs and throat? "Mommy?" She swallowed hard. "Are you . . . is it . . . okay?"

"Yes," the soft voice answered. And Sara was somehow taller, as if, unbent by illness, she could stand straighter than ever. Her eyes were not the warm golden brown Alex remembered. They were the duller brown of sparrow's wings, and watery. Had she been crying? And her skin, it had been so gray and drawn just before she died. Although Alex couldn't make out her features clearly, the woman before her had a smooth sheen to her skin, a translucency. Alex had the overwhelming urge to run to her. It would take only one giant step, one leap outside the circle. . . .

"She'll leave if you do." Mike squeezed her hand again. "It's not allowed."

Alex had seen only one other spirit. Her grandmother Leila, who was not exactly the kind of ghost you wanted to get close to. But Sara! Alex scoured her mother's face, wondering, did she remember all they'd done and had together, would she call her by her cherished childhood nickname —

"Lexi . . ." the spirit whispered.

No. Allie had been Sara's name for her. Could she have forgotten? Alex fought her quick disappointment. She knew so little about what happened to a person after . . . what they remembered or forgot. "Mommy," she said, "I have so much to tell you, to ask you —"

"We have little time. I can't stay long," Sara warned without smiling.

Alex took a deep breath. "I'm okay. I hope you weren't worrying, because everything worked out. I have a twin. Did you know?"

There was no answer. Alex said softly, "I'm safe, Mommy."

"I never doubted it. You are a strong girl, Alexandra. I always had faith in you. You must listen now, I have things to tell you."

"Wait, okay?" Alex couldn't help interrupting. There was something she'd wanted to say ever since Sara's death. The words caught in her throat now, choking her. But she had to get them out. "I'm sorry that I couldn't save you. I didn't know then all the stuff I know now. I didn't know how to help. But soon I'll be able to do more —"

A thin arm shot out from the spirit's cowled sleeve. Sara put her hand up as if to silence her daughter. But the floodgates had opened and Alex couldn't stop. Bursting into tears, gulping and sobbing, she said, "I was only fourteen. And I didn't know how to save you. Mommy, I'm so sorry."

"You waste your time feeling sorry for yourself," the spirit unexpectedly admonished.

Alex was stunned. "No," she managed. "Not for myself, for you —"

"It's too late for me, Alexandra, but there are others who need you. Who call out for you even now. I hear them every day. You have the power to heal so many mortal souls, but they are too far away. The longer you stay here, the more harm you do."

What was Sara telling her? She was hurting people, shirking her helping and healing duty, by staying in Marble Bay?

The spirit nodded.

But this was where she lived now. With Dave and Emily, who'd taken her in; with Dylan, the brother she'd bonded with; and especially with Cam, the sister she needed. And Cade. He'd come back to Marble Bay just to be with her.

In life, Sara could not read Alex's mind. She didn't have to; she'd always known her daughter's heart. Now she said sternly, "You must not allow your feelings to prevent you from doing what you were born to do. Not even for him, this boy."

She knew about Cade?

"You must leave the home of those who took you in," Sara told her. "They are good people, but they are not your destiny. You are needed elsewhere."

Chills shuddered through Alex. Sara was telling her to go to Coventry —

"No, not the island. You are needed at home. In the place we lived together. That was my charge when I was chosen as your protector. You must return to Montana. Soon."

Alex couldn't believe what she was hearing. It had

blindsided her, come out of left field. Her tears started up again, though she bit her lip trying to hold them back. Finally, she said, "Is that what you want me to do?"

"It is," Sara said with seething certainty, "what you were born to do. And, yes, it is my wish."

Alex fell to her knees and reached out. Hoping to touch her mother, she leaned forward, stretching her arms as far as she could. But there was nothing where the robed spirit had stood. Sara was gone.

CHAPTER THIRTEEN
THANTOS IN LOVE

He'd saved her life. Cam had little choice but to grant the lord of the manor an audience — of one. Miranda, he'd made clear, was not to attend.

Cam's ragged condition on her return to Crailmore had alarmed her birth mother. Miranda blamed herself for not sensing her daughter's perilous predicament. She'd begun to believe that her powers, once unrivaled, then lost, had at last returned. Cam's condition not only tore at her heart but devastated her fragile confidence.

Cam's own faith had been dealt a serious blow. She and Alex were supposedly born to be the most powerful witches ever. Yeah, right. So how come she couldn't even save herself? Not even when she'd had advance warning, had a vision, seen it coming! Was that how it would always be? Without Alex her powers would be halved? Without Alex she was not so extraordinary after all?

Cam sat rigidly in a wing chair in the salon of the mansion. Her back was to the fireplace, over which was hung the massive portrait of the family patriarch, Jacob DuBaer. On her first visit to Crailmore, Cam had heard conflicting tales of this commanding warlock. A physician by training, Jacob had survived the Salem witch trials. Thantos revered him; Ileana reviled him. Cam didn't know what to think.

Jacob's descendant, in his black trousers and black silk shirt, his hobnail boots resting on a brocade footstool, sat directly across from her — no less intimidating than the portrait of his forebear. Thantos overwhelmed the very chair he was in. His fingers were forming a tent just below his black-bearded chin. He was studying her and surely must have known that his intense scrutiny was making her uncomfortable.

Finally, he began. "What must you think of me, Apolla, in view of the poison that's been fed to you?"

Cam leveled her gaze at him. Tongues of flame reflecting from the fireplace shone in his coal-black eyes. It was summer yet the fire in the hearth was lit — which seemed reasonable, Cam thought, considering the icy coldness her uncle displayed. She tried not to glare at him. *What must I think of you,* she echoed silently. *I think you're a snake and a murderer. Fredo may have done the actual execution of my father, but somehow, someway, he was acting for you.*

Thantos, of course, intercepted the thought and smirked. "You've been taught to hate me since the day you learned of my existence," he reminded her. "But ask yourself this: If I am the murdering snake you'd have me be, why isn't your mother afraid of me? My dear brother Aron was not just your father, he was Miranda's husband. And she trusts me."

Cam didn't know. And it was not the first time she'd wondered about it.

Ileana, his own daughter, believed Thantos DuBaer was evil incarnate. Miranda, his widowed sister-in-law, regarded him highly, was grateful to him, had elected to live under his roof. These were strong, passionate, smart women, dedicated to the protection and nurture of the twins and to the benevolent Coventry credo. How could they clash so vehemently over the character of this frightening man?

Thantos crossed his long legs. "I don't claim to know why you are here now. But I choose to take it as a sign."

"Of what?"

The hulking tracker cleared his throat. "This is difficult for someone in my position to admit. But I have not always been the best . . . well, man I could be, or wanted to be. I have not always acted fairly toward —"

"— your daughter?" Cam interrupted.

"I knew you'd bring that up. Ileana is bitter; she has every right to be."

Cam arched her eyebrows. *Ya think?*

Her insolence had definitely annoyed him. "There were reasons, complications you can't possibly understand," he shot back at her. "Not yet. Soon you will learn more. You have my word on that."

Your word. Which is worth —?

He tilted his head and regarded her sternly. Even if she could have tapped into his mind, she didn't have to. It was easy to see what he was thinking: This was supposed to be the passive twin, the easily influenced one?

Thantos held his temper in check. "I want things to be better. I want the best for you. I always have."

"You have a strange way of showing it," Cam shot back. "Or am I expected to forget all the times you tried to snatch us, lure us, trick us, kill us?"

The tracker drummed his fingers on the arm of his chair. His voice rose. "I'm not a patient man, Apolla. If I'd wanted you dead, I could have left you in the quicksand.

If I really wanted to kill you, I would have. I've had the opportunity many times."

"Just not the success," Cam contradicted. "You were foiled every time by Ileana and Lord Karsh."

"We had a deal," he angrily reminded her. "You were to listen to me. Without prejudice."

Cam cupped her ears and cocked her head. "I'm all ears," she chided him.

"You mock me!" Thantos sprang up and hovered over her. "This is how you thank me for saving your life?"

If he expected her to cower at his outburst, he was wrong. Cam merely apologized.

Her uncle strode to the fireplace and stared at the portrait of Jacob DuBaer. Without turning from his austere ancestor, he spoke quietly, but deliberately. "There's something . . . a secret I've held close to my heart for many, many years. I want to share it with you now."

Was this the same important thing Miranda had been talking about? The one she and Ileana would not reveal until Alex got there?

Breaking into her thoughts again, Thantos spun and said, "Your sister needn't be here. You're the one I want to tell."

Now he had Cam's attention.

"On the day you were born, the tragic day your father was killed, I swore to take care of his family in every possible way. You were stolen, taken from me, but thankfully, I was able to fulfill that promise for Miranda. I arranged the best care money could buy for your devastated mother. For all these years, I never once wavered in my duty."

"My mother believed we were dead, that's why it took all those years for her to be healed," Cam challenged softly. "Only you knew we weren't dead."

"I knew nothing of the sort!" he thundered, losing it. "Karsh was wily. He had ways of keeping me in the dark about your fate. It was years before I learned you were alive. I vowed to find you, bring you together — no matter how long it took."

Someone suddenly came into the room and spoke. "Isn't it convenient, then, that while they were 'missing,' you took the next decade to run the DuBaer dynasty, to put your stamp on it. How deliciously pernicious."

Thantos and Cam whirled toward the intruder.

Ileana had returned. The majestic, mercurial blond witch dropped her suitcase on the floor with a deliberate thud. And shot Thantos a look of pure venom.

He narrowed his eyes. "This is a private conversation, Ileana. Leave."

"Leave? I only just arrived. Called back from my vacation early. I see why." She folded her arms defiantly.

Thantos ordered Cam, "Tell her this is between the two of us."

Cam was surprised and more than glad to see her guardian, but Ileana's timing couldn't have been worse. She'd interrupted the most interesting conversation — and the longest — Cam had ever had with her fearsome uncle. Whether he was telling the truth or spinning a web of lies, it seemed important to hear what their nemesis had to say.

"You read Apolla's mind," Thantos growled. "Or are your undependable powers on the fritz again? Don't let the door hit you on your way out."

Ileana's gray eyes connected momentarily with Cam's. Then she turned abruptly and stalked out, slamming the door behind her.

"She's jealous, of course. Always *has* been of the attention you and your sister receive." Thantos dismissed his daughter and resumed his monologue. "Through the years of Miranda's medical confinement, we became . . . close. Picture it, Apolla. I was her only visitor, caring for her, talking to her, trying to keep her spirits up, even in the most desperate times. Then something happened —"

"You were the only one who knew where she was, or even that she was alive!" Cam burst in angrily.

"I fell," Thantos continued, unfazed, "I . . . fell in love with her."

What? Cam went slack-jawed. No way! She had so not heard that.

"Miranda, alas, did not return my affection. How could she? My beloved was in mourning." The tracker began to pace the room. "For her dead husband, her daughters. She needed to be healed, to be reunited with her lost babies. I made that my life's work. It took longer than it should have only because, as you so adroitly pointed out, Karsh and Ileana blocked my way every time. Finally, I got my chance through that girl . . . that friend of yours . . ."

What girl? Cam was completely confused.

"The sickly wraith, the skinny girl," Thantos said impatiently. "I had her placed in the same clinic as Miranda, knowing they would meet. Once Miranda discovered the connection, there was nothing Karsh or Ileana could do to stop me."

Cam shook her head trying to clear it. Her friend Brianna had become anorexic, and gone into a clinic. Thantos was saying *he* deliberately placed her where Miranda was? How could that be? Instantly, Cam answered her own question. He'd gotten to Brianna's movie producer father through Brice Stanley, once a Coventry-bred warlock, now a bona fide Hollywood movie star. Brice had recommended the California clinic to Bree's dad.

"But how did you know Bree needed . . . care?" Cam challenged, feeling creepy and invaded. "Were you watching me? Watching Alex and me and our friends . . . clocking our every . . ." Shaken, she trailed off.

"Never underestimate me, Apolla, never," Thantos roared unexpectedly.

His deep voice boomed through the high-ceilinged room, making Cam jump, making her heart race with fear. Light-headed and hyperventilating, she couldn't listen anymore. While her uncle blustered on, she tried to digest what she'd already heard —

Frustrated, after a moment he shook her by the shoulders. "I will marry your mother," he said clearly, coldly. "You will help bring us together. We will be a family, Apolla. My family."

Ileana had walked out, but not away. Just outside the door, she pressed her back against the wall, hanging on her vile father's every word. She hadn't summoned Miranda to join her eavesdropping; it would have meant missing some part of Thantos's stunning speech. Ah, but she almost wished she had run and gotten the twins' mother.

He loved Miranda! What a crock. Thantos was merely but masterfully manipulating Cam, attempting to lure her to his side — and keep Miranda there, too. This was nothing but another devious scam to worm his way into Camryn's goodwill, to force the girl to doubt everything Ileana and Karsh had taught her.

Surely Camryn would reject this balderdash. Surely she could see the lying schemer for what he was. A power-mad warlock who would stop at nothing to get what he wanted: complete control over the rich and revered DuBaer dynasty.

But it was not his to have. Lord Karsh's journal had made that clear. Control of the family and its fortune was to pass into the hands of Aron's daughters.

Oh, he was good, that father of hers, Ileana mused, fuming. But so was she. He'd refused to raise or even acknowledge her. But she had his blood, his DNA, and she could be every bit as crafty.

What she must not do, she realized, was allow her fury, her righteous rage, to weaken her. Time and again, Karsh had cautioned her about that. And Karsh, the beloved warlock who had reared Ileana, had made her the guardian of the twins for just this reason. Not simply to protect and serve them, but for her to learn how to master her quick and violent emotions.

Well, she would do the memory of the wise old warlock proud. She would, indeed, protect Cam from the most serious threat she had yet encountered. And she would proceed cautiously, pounce when the time was right. Not now, not yet.

Ileana took a round gold coin etched with a dancing bear out of her pocket. As Cam — who looked like she was in a trance — left the salon, Ileana slipped it into the girl's palm. The DuBaer family amulet held great power. Cam would need it.

CHAPTER FOURTEEN
HELLO, I MUST BE GOING

She was lost when she should have been found; weighed down when she'd expected to feel lighter; poor when she'd hoped to be enriched. It was morning when Alex stumbled back home. Closure had left her an open wound.

She'd been granted a miracle. She'd gotten the chance to see Sara again — and to assure her single mom that the daughter she'd left behind was safe, secure, doing well. She'd been able to ask for forgiveness, to let go of the guilt plaguing her for not being able to save her mother's life.

Redemption. Asked and granted.

Nothing came for free, though. Hadn't Sara taught her that? There had been a high price for today's otherworldly visit. It had forced Alex to look at her new life and admit to herself that she appreciated and even loved much of it.

Now her dead mother was telling her she had to leave it all behind.

Alex was not analytical. She rarely waited to figure things out before acting. Cam was the patient, think-it-through sister. But as she dragged herself up the lushly carpeted staircase to their room, Alex tried to find her inner Cam. She needed to reason like her twin.

Once inside, she grabbed a spiral-bound notebook from her backpack and flopped down on her bed. She headed the first page *I know this much is true.*

Karsh had brought her here to Marble Bay, to the Barneses. The beloved old warlock had her best interests at heart. He'd been protecting her since the day she was born.

If it had really been her destiny to stay behind after Sara died, to work her magick in Montana, why had he moved her across the country and deposited her here?

One year ago.

Was that it, then?

She'd gotten only a year to connect with Cam?

Twelve measly months to find out who she was and sample the life she was destined for — before returning to Crow Creek.

Exhausted, Alex closed the notebook, let the pen drop to the floor, and picked up the phone. It was only five A.M. in Montana, but she had a lot to do. Alex *had* been keeping up with her Montana buds. Especially in the beginning. But maybe not so much lately, she thought guiltily.

Alex dialed her old friend Lucinda. Just to touch base, she told herself, just to hear Luce's bubbly voice again.

She knew at the first ring that she would not dump on her bud about what had gone down yesterday. How could she? What could she possibly say that wouldn't sound like she'd gone mental?

Once Alex assured the surprised girl she wasn't dreaming, and that no, nothing was wrong, Lucinda got her chatterbox on.

She was totally psyched to hear from Als and demanded to know every single "thingle" about Cade — except that she couldn't help breaking into blab about Andy Yatz, her once-and-forever crush. Still her old upbeat, uncomplicated self, Luce made Alex laugh, and made her homesick a little, too, dishing about Big Sky Frontier Town, the amusement park where Alex used to work. "Business is up," Luce informed her. "Lot of people are staying home, boning up on Americana — like this place ever represented the real thing!"

Phony or not, the theme park had finally raised Luce's paltry salary. Not much, but enough for her to start putting something away for college. Lucinda had always been a dreamer. These days, it looked like the girl was working to make her dreams come true.

They gabbed for over an hour. Then Alex woke her next victim: Evan, the boy from yesterday, the friend for always.

Dreadlock boy was doing amazingly well. His mom, a recovering alcoholic, had been sober for several months, gainfully employed, and happier than ever. Like Luce, Ev still worked at Big Sky, collecting summer coin to help pay the rent, with a little something left over for a new used guitar. There was a girl, too, Evan told her shyly.

Doris Bass, the town librarian and a true family friend, had been up for hours by the time Alex reached her. She was tickled to hear from "the library's former best source of revenue — the winner of the most late-book fines in town." Cheerfully, she told Alex that money had been pumped into Crow Creek from the government as part of rural reconstruction, and from private industry, too. There were more jobs to be had. The surplus in the town till was slated for upgrading the schools.

Everyone sounded hopeful.

Crow Creek, Montana, needed Alex? Less than ever. Still . . .

The last call she made before showering and dressing was to PITS. Only her second day at work and already she was calling in late.

"Yo, Dilbert." Alex punctuated her tease by knocking hard enough on Cade's cubicle to shake the corrugated wallboards.

She'd startled him by showing up at his job unannounced. Instead of being flustered, his face registered pure delight. He gave as good as he got, a quip-pro-quo comeback. "Yo, purple princess, how'd you get through security?"

"Got nothing to hide." She raised her arms and turned to show off her lavender tank top, threadbare jeans, and plum-colored moccasins.

"I get it," he teased. "You dazzled the rent-a-cops."

She blushed unexpectedly. Then went from pink to crimson when, impulsively, Cade wrapped his arm around her waist, pulled her to him, and kissed her.

Alex caught her breath. "We need to talk."

He arched his eyebrows. "Uh-oh, this can't be good."

Right. She probably shouldn't have opened with that. Few sentences started that way and ended on an up note. She slipped her arm around his waist. Color him warned.

"I'm gonna guess we need privacy," he surmised, leading her away from cubicle nation. "I have it on good authority that Luke McDonald is out on a long lunch break. We can use his office. I'm sure he won't mind, if all we're doing is talking."

With a sigh of regret, Alex confirmed that it was. Just talk. She knew what she had to tell him. She just hadn't planned how.

Cade's immediate clan, she knew, consisted of his dad and older sister — no mom in the picture. She died when he was about six, he had told her. Cade's dad pretty much brought the kids up on his own. He was a really cool guy, Cade had told her.

"Cade," she now began earnestly, "if you could talk to her . . . your mom . . . one more time, what would you say?"

Cade's face registered surprise. "Talk to her? You mean, like in a séance, or through a psychic? That whole 'other side' thing?"

Sort of, sort of not. Alex nodded. "Is there something you always wanted to ask her, or to tell her?"

Cade shrugged. "Not really. I was so little when she

died — not like your situation. Anyway, I don't believe in all that stuff. I think it's a scam, playing on people's weaknesses."

"Really?"

"Sure. When you lose someone you love, you're naturally vulnerable and needy. So a direct connect to the land-of-the-lost sounds incredibly cool. People want to believe so badly, that they're easily conned, swindled out of their money. Me? I believe when you're dead, you're dead. Want to grab some lunch?"

Of course Cade would think that. He wasn't a warlock. To him, the whole idea of communing with spirits was nothing but a scam.

Alex had come to the fork in the road. She'd known it would be there but hadn't wanted to reach it. She was a witch, he wasn't. She struggled with what to do next. She hedged. "I had a dream about my mom last night. A really . . . *vivid* one."

"Okay," he said, waiting for her to go on.

"She . . . she, um, suggested . . ." Alex couldn't look him in the eye. "No, she told me . . ." Alex dropped her head and stared at her gross, bitten fingernails. "That I need to go back . . . go home to Montana. Soon."

There was silence. Her voice barely above a whisper, Alex said, "I'm going, Cade. Back to Montana." Cade was flabbergasted.

"So what, you dreamed that she told you to split, and you . . . believe it? You're joking, right? You've been here a year. You've got a new family, friends, school. And I know it's not about me, but I just got here, Alex. I thought we had something."

We do have something! she wanted to scream. *Only sometimes, something isn't enough.*

She looked up at him and immediately wanted to cry. His blue eyes were searching her face, trying to figure out whether she was serious or playing him. Either way, he looked wounded.

There was one thing she had to know. "Were you planning to stay, after the summer? Would your dad even let you?"

Now *he* looked away, stared blindly at Luke McDonald's wall of framed credentials and pics of the corporate vice president posing with celebs. "Honestly, Allie?" Cade nervously rubbed his palms together. "I don't know. I figured it was a bridge I'd cross when we got there." He turned back to her and asked hopefully, "Are we there yet?"

"So you didn't register for school or anything?" she persisted.

Cade began pacing the office. "Alex, whether I stay or not shouldn't have anything to do with you leaving. I mean, going off because of some dream . . . Do you even know how crazy that sounds?"

Act One: Alex goes nuts in Mariner's Park, confusing Michaelina's ragging for Cade's thoughts. Act Two: Alex goes mental again, believing her dead mother is issuing life-changing orders.

"I know," she acknowledged, "but it might be soon. I might be going soon."

She was unprepared for his next comment, for the connection he made. "That girl, Michaelina — she have anything to do with this sudden urge to skip town?"

"Why would you think that?" Alex asked.

He shrugged. "Dunno. Just a hunch." Cade cupped her chin. "Listen. I trust my instincts. And my instincts tell me that girl is not to be trusted."

Alex turned her head, forcing him to drop his hand. "She's the first friend I've had on my own since coming to live here."

He was hurt. "What about me?"

She could have gone in to work. If she'd gone straight there from Cade's office, she wouldn't have been that late. Alex went home instead. Contacting Cam could not wait any longer. Telepathy hadn't worked, so Alex went for a method that had. She and Cam knew Ileana's e-mail address. Alex would send a message through her.

She flipped on Cam's computer, went online, and noticed something odd. The monitor displayed the last address Cam had used and the list of messages she'd sent and received before jetting off to Coventry.

It wasn't the regular *cambie@mb.com*. Her sister had a secret account.

It took less than a minute for Alex to wonder if she should honor Cam's privacy or click open her twin's recent e-mails.

Snooper won, hands down.

The password was a no-brainer. Same one Cam used on her normal account. But the list of senders on *apolla@mb.com* was anything but. Alex hacked in righteously.

The e-mails, all from one person, didn't surprise her, they made her sad. Then angry. How easy was it to see that Shane had been duping her sister? The whole bit about 'I need you, come back to Coventry.' Scam city! The boy was still bad to the bone.

For a nano, Alex hit the cynical brakes. Possible she was overreacting? Too much in touch with her inner Ileana, the wary witch who trusted no one? Possible that Shane honestly wanted to reform, truly needed a Cam-dose to do it?

Nah.

Anyone who wasn't Cam could see what a pack of lies he'd perpetrated.

That's when Alex and the truth collided, head-on.

Anyone who wasn't *Alex* could see that Michaelina had told her the same exact help-me-reform story. It was too, too obvious. Even Cade, nonwarlock, nonbeliever, knew a fraud when he saw one.

Cam had been gullible-girl? So had she. Which led Alex to the next connection. Whatever danger Cam had been in, he was behind it. Shane. What kind of peril was Michaelina leading *her* into?

Alex wasn't about to wait to find out. Right now, she had to reach her sister. Montana could wait. Cam could not. And then the phone rang.

CHAPTER FIFTEEN
CAM'S REVENGE

Face-time with Uncle Thantos had left Cam reeling, emotionally KO-ed.

She'd heard, without processing, everything he'd gone on about:

The stellar job he'd done running the family business, building it into the dynasty Aron would have wanted. How Thantos had abided by his brother's wishes for DuBaer Industries to be a force for good in the world. Did she know, by the way, it was he who had supplied every citizen on Coventry with a computer? The largesse of Thantos DuBaer, according to Thantos DuBaer, was unrivaled.

It could be bigger, better, more powerful, he humbly suggested, if Miranda were to marry him. And Camryn would agree to live with them, to be a family.

"Alex," Cam had said tonelessly. "You forgot Alex."

"Yes, of course Alex," the black-bearded tracker had agreed impatiently. "It goes without saying."

Trying to deal with her uncle's info overload, Cam had stumbled out of the salon, barely noticing Ileana furtively waiting outside. She felt rather than heard Ileana promise, "We're getting Alex. She'll be here soon. Be patient. Wait until Miranda and I have had a chance to tell you — to show you — what you need to know."

Ileana had pressed a coin into her hand. Cam didn't look at it. She went to splash cold water on her face. It wasn't until she reached to turn on the faucet that the round gold piece tumbled from her fist. She recognized the image stamped into it. The crowned bear was the DuBaer family crest. And she knew, intuitively, that the amulet was as powerful as the sun charm her father had fashioned for her.

Cam skipped dinner that night. She had no appetite. It was all she could do to drag herself to the computer in the Crailmore library. Logging onto e-mail, she typed a short and urgent message: Alex, I need you.

Then she'd gone to Aron's boyhood room and fallen into a deep, dreamless sleep.

She didn't hear Shane's telepathic message. She didn't know that he'd tried to see her and been turned away by one of Crailmore's staff. The first she knew of his visit was a message on her breakfast tray the next morning.

I have to talk to you. It's urgent. Meet me outside the gates. I will wait all day if I have to.

Cam pushed the tray away, fighting the urge to fall back to sleep. TMI. Too much information. It was important, she knew, to think through what she'd been told. But where to begin?

Thantos's shocking admission that he loved Miranda? And that he wanted Cam's . . . what? Her blessing? Her consent? Her help in bringing them together?

Or was it his casual admission that he could control the twins' lives? Exhibit A: Thantos had masterminded the meeting of Bree and Miranda.

And what of Cam's near-death experience in the quicksand? How had Thantos managed to show up in the nick of time and become her avenging hero?

It was some time after noon when she finally got dressed. Crailmore seemed to be empty but for the servants. There was no return e-mail from Alex in the library. There was no sign of her mother or her uncle anywhere. Ileana, she assumed, had probably returned to her cottage.

Cam thought briefly about going there. She was at the door, ready to leave Crailmore, when a thought halted her progress. What if . . . ?

What if anything Thantos said had even a grain of truth to it? Ileana's hatred of him eliminated her as an impartial sounding board.

"You can tell me. I would listen," a voice said.

Cam looked up abruptly. She'd walked out the door and was approaching the gates of the estate and there was Shane. True to his word, puppy-dog eyes full of remorse, he was waiting for her.

"No," she started.

He put up his hands in a gesture that was half surrender and half a plea for her to stop. "Please. I have to talk to you. It's about yesterday —"

"You mean the yesterday when you told me how safe I'd be or the yesterday when you didn't make a move to save me?"

He hung his head, looking appealingly defeated. "You'll never believe me, I know. But it was Sersee —"

Feeling almost ashamed of her gullibility and of her untamed heart, Cam swung back one of the tall gates and allowed Shane to enter the grounds — which was where she intended to stay, no matter what he might say this time.

"What was Sersee?" she prodded him. It appalled

her to realize that while she no longer trusted Shane she was still attracted to the treacherous warlock.

He leaped at the chance to explain. "It took me half the night, but I finally got her under a powerful truth-telling spell, and she spilled it all."

A sickening feeling, familiar now, came over Cam. Before Shane spoke, she knew what he was going to tell her. She saw it happening. But this vision was oddly blurred, as if washed over with a gray haze.

Her tumble backward into the pond had been no accident, he explained. It had been a trap set by Sersee. Of course the evil and envious witch knew about the quicksand. Last night she'd bragged to Shane that when she separated Cam from him, when she'd insisted on talking to Cam privately, she had used a potent spell to ease Cam's distrust and play on her fair-mindedness. She'd forced "the clueless mainlander" to give her the benefit of the doubt. And then had drawn Cam like a magnet into the fatal scheme.

At the same time, Shane insisted, Sersee had put a paralyzing spell on him so that he could not interfere with her deadly plan. And she claimed to have dosed the others, including her poor apprentice, Epie, with a mixture of herbs to confuse and confound them.

But Sersee hadn't counted on Thantos.

Through the strange grayish wash, Cam saw them

together — the huge and horribly grinning tracker and the cowering young witch.

Why had the most self-centered warlock on Coventry come to her rescue?

Shane reminded her: "You called out for someone who loves you."

Cam's jaw dropped. In her wildest dreams she would not have put Thantos on that list.

"I have an idea." His remorseful eyes glinted suddenly with mischief. "You could get revenge on her. You're a powerful witch. You owe it to her — after all she's done."

Cam shook her head, shook off the strange vision she'd experienced. A powerful witch? Not without Alex.

Shane read her mind and kissed her forehead. "Your sister isn't here, but I am," he whispered, "and I'd love to get revenge on Sersee. She made me helpless, unable to save you. I hate her for that."

The words *revenge* and *hate* jumped out at Cam, as if he'd boldfaced them. "No," she said softly. "That's not what our powers are for. You know that."

"Sersee tried to kill you, Cam. Twice now. She lied to you, betrayed you, stabbed you in the back. Besides," he prattled on before she could stop him, "what I have in mind won't end her life. She might not want to live, but she will."

*   *   *

Cam had mulled over Shane's plan from the time he'd gone to fetch Sersee until this very minute when she could hear the bell on the front gate ringing, indicating that her guests had arrived.

She had changed her mind a hundred times while waiting for them. One moment she'd judged the warlock's idea wrong and unworthy, and the next, she'd thought of it with a strange rush of energy — uncomfortable but exciting; a force that didn't come from her sun charm or her noble heritage but was fueled by a vengeful glee.

Still undecided, Cam opened the door to allow Shane and Sersee in. One look at the raven-haired witch's haughty scowl did the trick. Two could play mind games, she resolved. Mind and body games . . .

The decision to go along with Shane's idea left her feeling weird. Though her heart was pumping wildly, she experienced no fear. Her very nerves tingled with excitement and anticipation. And her mind seemed amazingly clear. *She is prideful and must be taught her place,* it insisted.

"Welcome to Crailmore," Cam heard herself say, as if from a distance. She was smiling, she knew, but the mad pulsing in her veins distracted her. She was suddenly eager, edgy, almost angry, as if her boiling blood were pumping pure adrenaline.

"Don't expect an apology," Sersee snarled, sweeping past her.

With clenched fists, Cam turned to study the shameless witch. Something was off about her. She was swathed in her trademark violet cape, but she seemed tired. In fact, Cam realized Sersee's eyes looked . . . brown?

"New contacts?" she asked, really curious.

Sersee tried to stop her hand flying to her mouth, but didn't quite make it. Cam wasn't supposed to have seen that. *I forgot to take them out!* She wasn't supposed to have heard that, either. But she did.

Quickly changing the subject, the unusually forgetful witch spun to face her. "You've made a speedy recovery. That's —"

"— disappointing?" Cam cut in.

Sersee scrunched her forehead. "You can't possibly think I wanted to see you harmed."

Not harmed, just dead, Cam thought, escorting Shane and Sersee through the great hall and up the tower stairs. They ended up in Aron's room — as planned.

Sersee was wandering around, picking things up, looking contemptuously at Aron's awards and certificates.

"My father wasn't just powerful," Cam said, "he was also very bright . . . yet humble, I'm told."

"Humble?" Sersee spun toward her and laughed. "He had every right to be, I'm sure. But powerful? I don't think so. Your revered father was, after all, murdered by his own brother, the weakest link in the DuBaer chain. Fredo was renowned as a certifiable moron."

"You don't think very much of humility, do you, Sersee?" Shane asked, smiling slyly.

"I don't think of it at all," she replied. "Humble pie is so not my dish."

"What is, then?" Cam demanded with the odd new fury building in her. "Conceit, smugness, arrogance?"

"All well earned," Sersee declared. "Where is your uncle? I didn't come all this way to visit with you."

"Your pride, Sersee," Cam observed, sticking to the script, "is as blown up, hollow, and full of hot air as a balloon."

Sersee's violet eyes — hidden behind the strange, sparrow-brown lenses — narrowed menacingly.

If Cam hadn't known what Shane was about to do — and if she weren't feeling so keyed up and capable . . . of anything — she might have been intimidated. As it was, she almost pitied the Coventry cur. Almost, but not quite.

Shane came at Sersee from behind, tossing just a

pinch of skullcap over her head. They wanted her still, not asleep. As the seeds rained down on the startled witch's ebony curls, Shane took Cam's hand. Together, they recited the incantation he had taught her.

> *You of no empathy, lacking in kindness,*
> *Must see yourself clearly, to cure you of*
> *blindness.*
> *Like a prideful balloon, be puffed up, we*
> *bequeath you,*
> *Till you lose your scorn for those you deem*
> *"beneath you."*

It was like watching a parade float being blown up.

Sersee's cape began to billow, wider and wider to accommodate her sudden horizontal growth spurt. Soon she looked like a waddling sphere. She didn't have to speak. Her horrified expression said it all. The fear and panic were as real and deep as anything Cam had seen or experienced, including her own near drowning.

Despite the warped exhilaration coursing through her, Cam was about to ask Shane to change Sersee back. But then the ever-expanding witch spat bitterly, "I wish you had died in that quicksand! I curse Thantos for rescuing you!"

"My, what a *huge* ego, and so *overblown*," Cam retorted, as she had practiced saying. "I'll get some transportation to take you home."

On cue, Amaryllis entered the room with a wheelbarrow.

"Up you go," Cam declared as she, Shane, and Amaryllis hoisted the supersized Sersee into the wagon. The sight of the jumbo Fury shaking with rage, sending layers of jellylike flesh quivering over the sides of the barrow, was supposed to be funny. At least Rowan and Serle seemed to think so when Shane invited the guffawing duo to wheel Sersee home.

The only one missing from the party was Epie. Had the girl been afraid to face Cam again after her treachery at the pond? Cam was about to ask Shane about it, when he stopped her with a triumphant hug. "Didn't I tell you revenge would be sweet?"

Mean-spirited laughter bubbled up inside her. It left an acid burn in her gut, an ulcer of spite. Sweet. Right, she thought. Sickeningly so.

And yet, watching the pain in Sersee's eyes when her so-called friends wheeled her down the path, a pitiful laughingstock, Cam did not feel sympathy or regret. She felt . . . powerful.

CHAPTER SIXTEEN
SPLIT DECISION

After Shane left, Cam lay trembling for a long time on Aron's big bed. The boiling exhilaration that had fueled her horrible behavior was seeping out of her — replaced by even hotter shame. No matter what the willful witch had done, what *she'd* done to Sersee was still wrong. Simple as that.

She couldn't bear to be in her father's room, to disgrace it with her presence. Disgust filled the vacuum her soul sickness left. Never would she have believed herself capable of such cruelty. She had crossed a line, passed over . . . to the dark side.

Cam felt an urgent need to be cleansed, to acknowledge what she had done, to tell on herself. She was still shaking as she got up. Her appalled brain searched for someone she could confess to and beg forgiveness from.

Not Miranda, not Ileana. She was too ashamed. Certainly not Thantos, who she suspected would be more pleased than revolted by what she'd done.

Who, then?

Karsh, of course —

Cam's momentary elation disappeared as she remembered that her steadfast friend was gone.

Before attending his funeral on Coventry, Cam had never seen a dead person. Her terror had dissolved the moment she'd set eyes on the ancient warlock, at peace in his plain pine coffin. His unlined face was smiling — or so it had seemed at the time. Even in death he'd continued to teach her, to show her what was to be feared and what was not.

She left Aron's room and asked Amaryllis for directions to the cemetery.

"Which one?" the servant had inquired, then hastily amended, "You must mean the DuBaer cemetery."

But when Cam told her who she wanted to visit, Amaryllis directed her to the southern portion of the island where the Antayus graveyard was located. There, among the simple plaques laid flat in the earth that marked the departed, Cam found the one she'd come for. She knelt beside it and brushed off bits of dirt that had blown onto the tablet. The new grass planted only weeks ago had started to poke though the fresh earth. Soon it would surround the old tracker's stone.

"Karsh," she whispered, as if that were the only way he might hear her, "I don't know who else to talk to. I know you're . . . well, not here anymore." Cam licked a salty tear that had trickled to the corner of her mouth. She sat beside the grave, hugged her knees, and poured her heart out.

"I'm so mixed up. I thought I finally understood who I was and what I had to do, thought I knew who was bad and who was good, and that I would always choose right over wrong. Now it's all turned inside out.

"You taught me to fear Thantos, who wanted us dead. But he says it's not true. He wants us to be a family. He says he loves my mother and wants to marry her so that we could be a family again. Karsh, is this what my father would have wanted?"

Cam sat there in solitude for a long time. She felt peaceful after a while. She'd gotten no real answers to her tortured doubts but realized it was important that she figure things out for herself. And knew, too, that she would, in time. She traced the name on the gravestone with her forefinger and voiced one last question.

"What I did to Sersee . . . it was terrible, I know.

But she tried to kill me, more than once. Didn't she deserve it?"

Cam shifted her weight and something crinkled in her pocket. It was a folded piece of paper that, when she unwrapped it, read: *An' it harm none, do what you will*.

Her father, as a schoolboy, had written that. Had Karsh, or his spirit, meant for her to find it just now? Was that his answer? Witches don't curse people, they don't make others suffer, they harm none.

She *had* harmed the girl.

Cam brushed the dirt from her pants. She would find Shane and undo the spell, return Sersee to her own body. It didn't matter what the diabolical witch had done. Neither Karsh, nor either of her parents, Aron or Miranda DuBaer, would have wanted her to seek revenge.

Cam was about to leave the cemetery, when her eye fell on the grave-marker just a few feet from Karsh's. Beatrice Hazlitt DuBaer. What was a DuBaer doing here? Weren't all of them laid to rest in the grander sanctuary on the other side of the island?

"My wife," someone said unexpectedly.

Cam spun around. "Thantos? What are —?"

"Looking for you," the burly tracker responded. "My staff told me I might find you here, and I wanted to be sure you hadn't gotten yourself into any other life-threatening situations." He eyed her, then chuckled. "I *am* capable of a joke, you know."

Cam gestured toward the plaque. "Was she Ileana's mother?"

He nodded. "She died in childbirth. She rests here because that was her wish. As hard as I tried, I could never make her feel like part of the family. She asked to be buried here, among her own kind."

"Is that why there are no pictures of her at Crailmore? No mementos . . ." And no one, she thought, ever spoke of this woman. But for this simple headstone, it was as if Beatrice DuBaer had never existed. Cam thought of Ileana. No wonder —

Thantos put his arm around her. Cam didn't flinch this time or make any move to pull away. "I heard what you did to the Tremaine girl." He was speaking of Sersee. "Good for you. A DuBaer does not allow herself to be taken advantage of —"

Cam was about to challenge that, when Thantos stopped and abruptly stood up. "We have company."

"Where *is* she, Thantos?" Ileana snapped, strikingly beautiful in her royal-blue cloak.

"How lovely of you to join us." Thantos looked right through his daughter, as if she didn't exist. It was Miranda, who stood behind Ileana, that he welcomed. "I was just telling Apolla about —"

Miranda cut him short. "We tried to find Alex. She's not where you said she'd be. Where is my daughter?" Her tone was suspicious, borderline nervous.

Cam felt a wave of panic. "Alex is missing?"

"No, no!" Thantos assured the women. "Of course she's not. Did you go to the —"

"We went everywhere you told us to," Miranda responded. "The Barncses' home, to that boy's house, to the apartment of the little Coventry girl —"

"The Coventry girl?" Cam tried to figure out who they meant.

"Her name is Michaelina," her mother answered. "She's one of the young witches who tormented you and Alex. She's now in Marble Bay, where she's befriended your sister. You didn't know?"

Marble Bay? How could that be possible if Michaelina was doing "community service" here?

Duh. Sersee had lied about that, too. How new.

"You sent us on a wild-goose chase," Ileana accused him. "If you've harmed her —"

Cam blurted, "No!"

Three pairs of eyes stared at her questioningly. But Cam responded with a question of her own. "If something bad happened to Alex, I'd know it. Wouldn't I?"

Miranda put her arm around Cam's shoulders. "I hope so."

Thantos rolled his eyes. "Oh, the lot of you! Come here. I'll show you where she is. From the inside pocket of his cape, he withdrew a gold lighter. He tossed a handful of herbs into the flame while reciting the Situator incantation.

There in the firelight, was Alex. She wasn't alone. Someone, Cam suspected Cade, was cupping her sister's chin. For a split second, Cam wondered if she should blow out the flame. If this was about to get R-rated, she was sure Alex would not want an audience. But just then, the vision faded.

"I'm going to get her," Miranda said decisively, turning to leave.

Thantos pulled her back. "Save your strength, Miranda. You just got back. Let me send a servant. It will be faster and not tiring for you."

Even Cam noticed that Thantos said nothing about Ileana. Did he have any feelings for her at all?

"No, in fact, he doesn't." To Cam's embarrassment, Ileana answered her silent question. "It's only appropriate that my father demonstrates his apathy for me as he stands at my mother's grave," Ileana continued. "He believed what Leila DuBaer told him — that Beatrice Hazlitt wasn't good enough for him. Not even in death would he have his wife — my mother — among the DuBaers."

Cam was puzzled. "But . . ." She turned to Thantos. "You said Beatrice asked to be buried here."

The statement set Ileana off; she went ballistic. Red-faced with rage, she turned on Thantos. "Is that what you told her?"

Miranda jumped in. "Calm down, wait . . . surely Thantos didn't —"

But Ileana would not be comforted. Her gale-force diatribe had only just begun. It was aimed at Cam. "Ask him, your dear uncle Thantos, to tell you the real reason he cast her out. Ask him to tell you about my mother's family, who 'her kind' were. Ask him to tell you why he married someone against his mother's wishes — and why he deserted me, his own flesh and blood. And then, Apolla, ask him how he dared usurp what isn't his. What is yours. And your sister's! And mine!"

Ileana now spun toward her father, glaring at him, daring him to respond. But he wasn't looking at her.

Cam was floored. It wasn't just the bile Ileana had spewed — she could barely follow that. It was the way Thantos had watched Miranda throughout his daughter's attack. He was studying her face, trying to gauge her reactions, her feelings.

Cam's mother was upset, but peacemaker was her default mode and she fell into it. She reached for Ileana, but the infuriated witch wasn't having it. To Thantos, Miranda said quietly, "You might have considered options other than casting the child out completely. No matter how much pain and sadness you were in."

Thantos drew himself up to his full, intimidating height. "I did what I thought safest and best. I was not in my right mind. I was crazy with grief over the death of my wife. It was my idea, after all, to place Ileana in the care of the good and wise Karsh."

It was Miranda's turn to gape. "Rubbish! That was Aron's idea, not yours."

Ileana gave a bitter laugh. "How surprising. You coopted an idea of Aron's — as you have all your life. You have always coveted everything he had — including his wife. And now his children."

Cam thought she was going to gag. She remembered the notes from Thantos's earliest teachers. *He's copying Aron again.* So . . . did Thantos not love Miranda? Had he been lying about that and about loving Cam?

The hulking tracker silenced her thoughts with a fierce look. She blinked but did not turn away. "Why was it best to place Ileana with Karsh?" she asked. "Why didn't you raise your own daughter?"

"He'll never tell you the truth," Ileana sneered. "He'll *say* he was not fit to be a father. But you can read for yourself. Lord Karsh wrote it down. All of it." Ileana untied her cape and took from a pouch beneath it an old leather-bound book. Cam could see that it was filled with parchment sheets. Where had she seen the volume before? Where had she seen the pages?

"No!" It was Miranda. "Not yet, Ileana. We decided. We would wait for Artemis."

So that was it. *That* was the big deal? She was not going to see Lord Karsh's writings without Alex. Cam kept her voice steady. But she knew what effect her words would have. "What's in there, Mother?"

Miranda paled. It was the first time Apolla had called her Mother. Whatever she'd meant to say fell away. The ethereally beautiful witch just folded, choked up. She could not answer her daughter.

But Ileana could. She held up the journal. "Your family history, that's what's in here. Your legacy, yours and Alex's. Your destiny."

"Or," Thantos bellowed so loudly, they all jumped. "Is it in here?"

They whirled as one, to see, in his large hard hands, an identical book.

CHAPTER SEVENTEEN
BETRAYAL BY FIRE

Alex was waiting for Ileana. Her guardian had put her on standby for a fast trip to Coventry. But she hadn't said exactly when liftoff would be. So when the phone rang, Alex jumped on it.

But it was Michaelina — trying to talk Alex into coming to work. Word of the "psychic waitresses" show at PITS had spread. Customers were requesting her. "So get in here. This is the land of tips aplenty."

"Enjoy," Alex responded. "I've got to go to —" She stopped. Trust Mike? Even Cade had advised against it. And he didn't know half the half-pint's tricks.

"But it's not time yet," Michaelina mused aloud. But it was her thoughts Alex heard, not her words. And they were panicked: *She can't have been called to the woods yet. Not without me being told.*

Did she mean Salem Woods, Alex wondered. Was the spirit of Sara supposed to get in touch with Michaelina before telling Alex it was time to return to Montana?

"Please, please," Michaelina begged. "You can't leave me here alone. The place is mobbed. It's not fair. You're the one who thought up working for Pie in the Sky. Just come by for a minute. Please. It's sooo important. I mean, I've got something for you. Something you need and will really, really like. You don't even have to come inside. I'll meet you out back."

"I can't stay," Alex warned the imp, intrigued despite her distrust.

"Outside," Mr. Tagliere told her twenty minutes later when she arrived at the pizza place. Motioning to the back door, he said, "She's on break. Been working hard today, double the load without you."

The rear door of PITS opened onto a set of metal stairs that led to the delivery alleyway. The day had turned dreary. The morning's light clouds had become thicker, threatening rain. Mike was sitting on the top step, counting a wad of bills.

Alex was impressed — and wary. "You made that much in only a few hours? What'd you do, turn the tables over every fifteen minutes?"

Mike grinned. "No need to rush our devoted patrons through their lunches. I used another kind of magick to build the Michaelina — and Alex — fund. Told ya I had something you needed."

Alex was afraid to ask. Who had Mike cheated, the customers or Mr. Tagliere?

"No one," she protested. "No one all that much, anyway." She claimed she'd written the checks accurately. But by the time they went into the cash register, they'd been . . . um . . . slightly altered. Less money due the restaurant, more money in Mike's pockets. A bill for twenty-four dollars with a five-dollar tip, she explained, had magickly changed to fourteen dollars for the till and ten for Mike . . . and, of course, for Alex, too, she added again. "I told you I had something you needed."

Alex was outraged. "How could you do that? I don't know about Coventry, but here on the mainland, that's stealing. It's a crime — punishable by law."

Michaelina tried to trump Alex's upset with self-righteousness. "I brought more customers in. They came to see me — and you. It's a game; it's entertaining. It's only fair that I get more of the proceeds."

"That's twisted. Besides, I may not be an initiated witch yet, but I know we're not supposed to use our powers to cheat people!"

Michaelina shrugged. "Here's a tip for you, free of

charge. Sometimes our powers are best served when we use them to serve ourselves."

Alex crossed her arms. "We're going back in there and you're giving Mr. Tag every last dime you owe him." She got up and was reaching for Michaelina's hand when a dizzy spell hobbled her. She gripped the handrail hard, to keep from fainting.

Arise, Artemis. The time is now. You are needed!

The voice was definitely not Ileana's. It sounded more like Sara's spirit had, but impatient and commanding.

Where am I needed? Who are you?

Michaelina stood next to Alex, clutching the railing just as hard, trembling. She, too, had heard the demand.

You don't recognize me? I'm Sara, your mother. I told you the time to leave would come quickly. Hurry now, get to the woods. The transporting spell is ready to be cast. It will take you . . . to where you are needed.

Alex knew that Mike would hear her telepathic response, but it couldn't be helped. *I can't go yet! I have to go to Coventry Island. Cam — Apolla — my twin sister is there, and Ileana is coming for me. I'm not ready —*

I will say when you are ready! the voice roared. *You have no choice, Artemis. You must go to the woods. I await you there.*

Quickly, Alex turned away from Michaelina and desperately willed her thoughts to be scrambled, secret, and undecipherable.

Because the voice was not Sara's.

If Alex had told Sara that someone needed her help, her mother would not just let her go, but urge her to. She would never have asked Alex to turn her back on the person, never have spoken to her so sternly. Whoever had called her, whatever she'd seen in Salem Woods, could not have been Sara Fielding or her ghost.

Alex was devastated. Her anger dampened by disappointment and heartbreak.

But who was this brash imposter? Only one way to find out.

She grabbed Michaelina's wrist and told the awe-struck pixie, "We're going to Salem. This time, you'll be paying the cab fare. You can afford it."

No matter what Alex said to her, Michaelina refused to stray from the same script she'd been reciting for days. She didn't know anything about Shane and Cam. She really was here looking for a second chance. She'd thought Alex would help her, be her friend. She had no idea why Alex had turned on her this way.

Mike's words were lies, but the fear in her emerald eyes was very, very real. Whatever was freaking her was her secret. She was much more skillful than Alex in scrambling her thoughts — and now whatever was scaring her was tucked safely away, out of Alex's reach.

It was daylight. The woods shouldn't have been as foreboding as they had been in the dead of night. Maybe it was the rain, then. The skies had opened, and inside the forest, it was dark, dreary, and muddy. The thick canopy of leaves overhead kept Alex and Mike from getting completely soaked. It was easy to find the exact spot they'd been to the day before: The circle was still there. The rain had not washed away the line Mike had cut into the earth; it remained defiantly deep and defined. Alex squinted at the thicket of trees where "Sara" had appeared hours ago. Was someone hidden in there now? She headed over but hadn't gotten very far when a voice cried out: "Get back! You must remain inside the circle."

Angrily, Alex retorted, "I refuse to stay inside the circle."

"Fine!" the ghostly voice snapped. And then a figure appeared from behind the trees. A large, round creature draped in what could have been a billowing, velvet tent. "The choice is yours, Artemis: You can die in these woods or obey my command and return to the circle."

Alex was too astonished to be angry. "Who are you? What are you? What do you want?"

The "spirit" tossed back the hood of her cloak. Alex gaped at the ebony curls — familiar, yet so out of place on the swollen thing before her.

"Sersee?" she whispered.

"You will obey me, Artemis DuBaer!" A sudden shock of flames erupted from the transformed witch's puffy hands. Alex staggered backward. Feeling seared and raw, she landed inside the circle, tumbling and falling. Sersee's heat wave had felled Michaelina, too. The tiny girl came to rest beside Alex, clearly not of her own free will.

Her face bright red and beginning to sweat, Mike gingerly picked herself up and glared at her sister Fury. "What are you doing in that flesh bag? She knows who you are. You can show yourself now." Sersee didn't answer, then Mike suddenly gasped, "Oh, no!" Then tried to hide her grin. "She *didn't!* You let Apolla DuBaer do this to you?"

"She had help," Sersee snarled. "Shane betrayed me. But have no doubt this is only temporary. As opposed to the spell I will work on the two of you — which will be quite permanent!"

"The two of us?" Mike's smile disappeared. "What's your issue with me? We were sent to get rid of *her.*"

Alex blinked at Michaelina, understanding dawning quickly. It had all been a scam! And not just to snare her. Sersee and company wanted two T*Witches for the price of one. Divide and conquer. Shane had lured Cam to Coventry. Mike had played the dead-mother card with Alex to send her far away to Montana. Sersee was involved in everything.

Alex didn't have to be told who was pulling their strings — but the bloated witch blurted it out, anyway.

"Oh, didn't you know?" Sersee taunted Michaelina. "My instructions from Lord Thantos were to get rid of both of you. I guess you didn't get that memo."

"At least I didn't *eat* that memo," the furious little witch shot back. "Or the one with the simple arithmetic. Two of us versus — well, it looks like you've doubled, but there's still only one of you —"

"Only one of me?" Sersee, her balloon face stretched taut, did her best to laugh. "Yes, just one — imbued with the dark magick Lord Thantos has granted me for my task. But now that little miss punk head knows the deal and refuses to play nice . . . I'm going to turn you both into the hot stuff you're not, and then commend your ashes to the wind."

Sersee had worn brown contact lenses when she was "impersonating" Sara. Now she focused her wild violet eyes on the ground at their feet. Instantly, in spite of the dampness left by the rain, the pine needles, leaves, and twigs on the forest floor began to smolder. Tiny flames erupted through the gathering smoke. They

175

formed a ring inside the "sacred circle," crackling and building as they flared closer and closer to Alex and Michaelina.

Smoke set Alex's eyes tearing. She couldn't focus them on anything, couldn't will a high branch or earth-bound stone to lift off and put the deadly witch out of business. Michaelina, coughing and choking in the smoke, was out of commission, too.

Before the trapped girls could come up with a counter spell, Sersee took her mission a step further. She had no plans to leave their demise to nature. She threw off her cloak, set it afire, and sent it flying telekinetically at the stranded witches, to smother them in flames.

Alex and Mike tried to duck, to move out of the way of the fiery missile, but the flames on the forest floor leaped up at them. There was nowhere to go and nothing to do but watch the lethal fireball careening at them.

"Please, Sers, please," Michaelina screamed, "I can reverse the curse! I can make you normal again!" It was a desperate lie and even Alex knew it.

Still, the cape *stopped* in midair!

But it wasn't Sersee who'd halted its flight. "Over my dead body!" a whiny voice intoned. A blast of arctic air tore at the burning cloak, sending it sailing overhead, over the tops of the trees toward the ocean. A second gust blew out the leaping ground flames. Through the dark smoke, Alex could make out a familiar figure, plump and angry, small eyes narrowed at Sersee.

"Epie!" Sersee gasped, clearly as startled as Alex and Mike. "You fool! How dare you?" Her fleshy hands tried to curl into fists but failed. "How did you find me? Who sent you here?"

"Guess," Epie insolently challenged.

"Thantos!" Alex and Sersee cried out at once.

"But why?" Mike chimed in, batting at her charred PITS apron, trying to quash the last stubborn flames.

"I know this will come as a blow to your bloated, and I do mean bloated, ego, Sers," Epie said, "but Thantos doesn't trust you any more than you ever trusted me. He sent me to spy on you, to make sure you did your job —"

"Then why, idiot, did you stop me?"

"Because of that! Because of the way you treat me! I thought you were my friend. But you're not. Lord Thantos told me that. He wanted me to kill you after you got rid of Alex and Mike. And I promised him I would. That's why he granted me the power to blow you into the sea, the same way you made me blow Camryn into the quicksand —"

"Cam!" Alex had heard enough. It was time to get to Coventry. She only hoped it wasn't too late.

"Don't you dare move!" Sersee shrieked at her. In her stretched-to-bursting purple gown, she looked like an angry grape.

"You're in no condition to stop me, Sersee. And no one else around here is going to, either." Alex glared menacingly at Epie and Mike.

Michaelina raised her hands in surrender. "I'm not going to stop you," she promised, "but you're not going to stop me, either. I'm going back to Coventry with you."

"And so am I," Epie insisted. Turning back to Sersee, she added, "I am over you and so outta here —"

"You're not going anyplace!" the swollen witch commanded. "At least not without me. I've got some serious scores to settle back home."

That made three enraged Furies accompanying Alex to Coventry Island. Epie and Mike were furious with Sersee. And Sersee wanted the treacherous bully Thantos dead.

One thing was very clear to Alex — there was no anger like that of a Fury foiled.

CHAPTER EIGHTEEN
LOVE IS BLIND

"Liar!" Ileana raged.

"Ingrate!" Thantos sneered.

"Desperate, deceitful beast! No matter what the Council judged, it was *you*, not Fredo, who was responsible for Aron's death!"

"And you who lured your beloved guardian, Karsh, to his death!"

"You dare to even mention his hallowed name! Hold your tongue before I turn it into a slug!"

"Even before you lost your powers, vixen, you could never put a spell on me. You are as spoiled, weak, and vain as your mother —"

Tracker versus guardian. Father versus daughter.

The face-off was as classic, Cam thought, as a great big Greek tragedy. Thantos's and Ileana's contempt for each other was so raw, so powerful, ran so deep, it hurt both Cam and Miranda to witness it.

"That journal is as phony as you are!" Ileana tried to wrench the book out of her father's hands. He lifted it easily out of her reach. "You turn a smiling face toward Miranda, who first you hid away in an insane asylum and then lied to for years. Lied about her children —"

"Silence, insolent witch!" Thantos turned on his hobnailed boots, his heavy dark cloak swung wide behind him, smacking his daughter and almost bowling her over. "Why do we wait for Artemis when Apolla is here?" he asked Miranda, as if he hadn't noticed Ileana stumbling backward in his wake. "Why don't we retire to Crailmore and study both books and see then which is the original and which an audacious fraud?"

Ileana raced after him, shouting, "Audacious fraud exactly. That's what you are! Why would Karsh give *you* the book?"

Before she could say any more, Thantos tossed a handful of herbs into the air and silently recited an incantation. The Traveler's spell, Cam remembered. And the next thing she knew, she and Miranda were with the black-bearded tracker in the massive salon at Crailmore.

"Where is Ileana?" Miranda demanded, putting a

protective arm around Cam's shoulders. "You must bring her here at once or we will leave."

"Miranda. Dear Miranda. When will you learn?" Thantos stalked over to his thronelike chair and threw himself dramatically into it, as if wounded by his sister-in-law's request. He shook his head sadly. "You are too trusting, too good to know the mischief of which your niece is capable."

To Cam's surprise and delight, Miranda glared at Thantos, changing her appeal to a command. "Bring Ileana to us now or we leave!"

With a theatrical sigh, the tracker stood and mumbled an incantation. At the end of it, he threw up his hands. Cam expected a blinding flash of light, maybe even smoke, and for Ileana to materialize dazed and bedraggled. It took a moment, and then the mercurial witch did appear — more furious than before.

"Ileana." Miranda stepped between the tracker and his enraged daughter. "What harm can come of it? Let us do what Lord Thantos has suggested. Let us compare the journals —"

"Excellent." Thantos smiled at Cam and Miranda. He placed his leather-bound book on his desk, opened its cover, and beckoned them near to inspect it. Inside was a sheaf of parchment pages covered with the crabbed handwriting that even Cam, on one of her brief visits to

Karsh's cottage some weeks ago, recognized as the wise warlock's. "Ah." Thantos beamed gratefully at Cam. "You know his hand. You know this is Lord Karsh's writing —"

"It's a forgery!" Ileana shouted, clutching the volume she owned to her chest.

"Is that so? Let us compare them." Although his words were civil, the tone he used on his daughter was contemptuous. When Ileana had placed her book beside his, Thantos laughed. "Come see, Miranda," he invited, flipping through the pages. "See this paltry attempt at copying Lord Karsh's handwriting, look how messy, how unsteady the last pages are —"

"Proof that it's genuine!" Ileana insisted. "He was at death's door. Of course his writing was shaky. It took the last of his strength to set it all down. To make certain everything was said and explained." Speaking of Karsh, remembering his whispered last words — "It is all written" — almost undid her.

"And, of course, you would have no reason to lie." Thantos's amused black eyes contradicted the taunting innocence with which he'd whimpered the question. As if snapping shut a trap, he added, "What reason indeed, I think we'll soon see."

Standing beside her mother, Cam studied both books. Their covers seemed identical — as alike as she and Alex. The title inscribed on the worn leather covers was *Forgiveness or Vengeance*. But inside they were different. In one, the parchment pages were bound into a book; in the other, Ileana's, a stack of parchment was hidden inside a hollowed-out volume. Both appeared to have been written with an ink pen — though there were more smudges on Ileana's pages than on Thantos's. Both books were of the same length and trailed off in the same spots. The handwriting differed only slightly, mostly in the last few entries.

Thantos flipped through both books, stopping in the same place in each, toward the end of the journals. Skimming the pages, it was clear that both books contained nearly identical information. The fact that Karsh Antayus and Nathaniel DuBaer — the twins' grandfather — had been best friends throughout their lives. They were closer than blood relations — that was without dispute, as was the claim that Nathaniel had confided to Karsh his dying wishes for his family.

After that, the two books differed.

According to the journal that her uncle had produced, Karsh had *confessed* to killing Nathaniel deep inside the caves of Coventry. *Stricken by a sudden rage, I murdered my dearest friend. An unpardonable act I must confess before I die. The curse,* he'd written, *turned out to be stronger than both of us.*

Could that be true, Cam wondered, feeling her heart

sink at the thought. Could kindly Karsh, the wise, protective warlock who had brought her and Alex together and guarded them vigilantly against all harm, could such a gentle man kill in a dark rage? Kill his best friend?

In the book Ileana owned, the scenario was slightly, but importantly, different. Karsh and Nathaniel had descended into the caves together, where Nathaniel became the victim of a deranged cave-dwelling warlock. And in a foiled attempt to save his dear friend's life, Karsh became the instrument of his death. But it had been an accident. In this version also, he referred to a curse.

But neither entry explained it. Whatever the curse was must have been described earlier in the books, Cam reasoned, or would be revealed later.

Ileana's gasp startled her. "There!" the furious witch shouted, pointing at her father's book. "There the poisonous lies begin! There is the reason for this monstrous counterfeit!"

Cam quickly read Thantos's passage.

My sons shall continue my legacy. All of them together, in their birth order, Thantos, Aron, and Fredo, shall lead the DuBaer dynasty into the next century. I have instilled in my sons all that is good, fair, and just. I have complete faith in them. If anyone can stop the Antayus curse, it is surely the next generation of DuBaer men.

Those were Nathaniel's dying words, according to Thantos's book.

Ileana's book told a different story.

"'From this day forward,'" she read aloud in a voice quavering with emotion, "'only *women* will decide the fate of the DuBaer dynasty. Remarkable women, dedicated to good, to compassion, and to justice, schooled in the ways of our craft, and free of the Antayus taint.'"

Turning to Cam and Miranda for acknowledgment, Ileana's face went from triumph to terror, shock, and outrage. "You don't believe me? Miranda Martine DuBaer! You saw this with your own eyes. You —"

"I saw the book you showed me. I had no reason to doubt its authenticity." Miranda looked away, lowered her head, unable to face Ileana. "But that was before I had knowledge of a second book. And, dear child, you bear your father such deep-seated hatred, is it possible *you* have the forgery? Is it possible you've done something . . . rash . . . something vengeful . . . to harm the man who abandoned you?"

Trying to suppress his gloating smile, Thantos pushed past his stunned daughter and laid a heavy arm around Miranda's slender shoulders. "We mustn't be too harsh," he crooned benevolently. "Resentment and retribution are not her choices but her nature."

The color drained from Ileana's beautiful face.

She'd begun to hyperventilate. Unable, it seemed, to catch her breath, she'd been rendered speechless.

But not for long. "Of course he would try to discredit me, make me out to be nothing but a vengeful fool, a liar without scruples or conscience!" The deeply wounded witch tried to contain her hurt and the hot tears that had begun to well in her extraordinary gray eyes. "But you, Miranda? You who have known me all my life — surely you know better. How can you believe I would invent such a grotesque lie?"

Anchored by Thantos's arm, Miranda hung her head, whether in confusion or shame, Cam couldn't tell. Suddenly, Ileana called her name. "Apolla! Camryn, don't you understand? 'This family, this too, too powerful dynasty' — it was our grandfather's wish that you and Artemis would lead it. Not me. Not with my mother's 'tainted' Antayus blood. But the daughters of Aron, you and your sister —"

"If that was what Lord Karsh meant," Thantos cut her off, with a mocking smile, "why would he have assigned as their guardian a rebellious, rageful child, a mere adolescent whom the whole community despaired of? Why not choose an Exalted Elder, someone wise and respected? No, Ileana. You are the living proof of your own lie!"

Cam felt a wild urge to cover her ears and shout,

"Enough!" Nothing made sense now. There was too much to think about, too many distorted versions of the same tale. Her instinct, her heart, was with Ileana, yet even Miranda could not endorse the excitable and overwrought witch's story.

Shell-shocked, Cam backed away. She'd come — was it less than a week ago? — for Shane. The wayward warlock had said he needed her. She'd come to help him. Finding a soul mate in the process, she'd told herself, might be a bonus.

Instead, every step she had taken on Coventry had exploded a land mine of secrets. Now she stared into the open wounds of a family battle. And if Ileana's version was the correct one, soon she'd be called upon — she and Alex — to rule . . . to lead the DuBaer dynasty?

"But this is madness!" Ileana burst out, her face now slick with tears. "Miranda, Camryn, you cannot seriously believe that I created this deeply detailed document out of sheer spite and malice. How could I? With what means? Do you honestly think I sat for days on end forging my beloved guardian's handwriting and distorting his will?"

Cam's eyes glazed; she saw something that wasn't in the room. "Are you all right?" her mother asked anxiously, rushing to her side. "Are you having a vision, a premonition?"

"No," Cam said slowly, "I'm remembering something."

Immediately, Thantos inserted himself between Miranda and Cam. He placed a calloused palm on her forehead, as though to check her temperature, to see if she had a fever.

Cam twisted away. Instinctively, she knew that his gesture, however caring it was supposed to be, served a darker purpose: to physically come between Cam and Miranda. To block them from each other. To stop Cam from describing what she had suddenly recalled.

All right, then, she thought. She would not spar verbally with her devious uncle or his distressed daughter. Instead, she asked, suggested, *insisted* that they follow her. Miranda agreed without hesitation. She was at Cam's side in a moment. Ileana, anxious and wary, trailed them. Thantos hung back.

"Apolla," he called out, "this is my home and I am the head of this family. You may not command in this house."

None of them paid attention to his blustering. And so the hulking tracker had to choose. He could stay behind sulking defiantly, or give in and go along with the women. He wavered. They were out the great room's doors before he decided to join them, his boots clacking angrily across the marble floor of the hallway.

"But this was my room!" he thundered, when Cam led them into his childhood bedroom. She went directly to the bureau and began to push it away from the wall. Miranda and Ileana watched wordlessly.

"What foolishness are you up to?" Thantos demanded.

"I discovered this by accident," Cam explained as the secret door came into sight, "and I went down —"

"Down the rabbit hole?" Thantos smirked sarcastically.

Cam spun around. "Down to the caves. I think you know what's there."

Thantos bristled, then laughed dismissively. "The rabbit hole, that's what we called it. A childhood playroom. I haven't thought about this place in years."

Cam had already entered the tunnel. Her uncle's voice echoed through the dark chamber. "There's nothing down there that has anything to do with this," he insisted impatiently.

"Nevertheless —" Cam heard Miranda say, then heard her delicate footsteps on the creaky spiral staircase, followed by Ileana's high-heeled tread.

"What new madness is this?" Thantos's voice reverberated as he reluctantly brought up the rear. "What do you hope to find in this dank and deserted place?"

"I think you know," Cam shot back over her shoulder as she entered the round cavern. And then she stopped, silenced by shock. The central cave and all five tunnels that radiated out of it were dusty, deserted, eerily quiet. There was no outcropping of stone, no hint of the rock formation that the ponytailed scribe had used as a desk, no telling globules of wax on the stone walls and floor to prove that candles had been lit here.

Thantos read her mind and loosed a bellowing laugh that shook the empty chamber. "It was foretold that you and your rebellious sister would become powerful witches," he sneered. "Yet you cannot tell the difference between a nightmare and an omen."

Cam was shaken. Could she have dreamed this? Had it been a vision — the first ever that had not come to pass?

"No!" The decisive voice was Ileana's. She, too, had heard Cam's thoughts. "Say it. Say what you saw. I believe you, Apolla!"

Miranda looked from Ileana to Thantos. And made her choice. "Daughter, I trust you with all my heart. Don't be afraid to speak."

"Right here, in this exact spot," Cam asserted, "I saw a boy, a scraggly-haired young warlock who was writing with a quill pen. The pages he had gathered looked just like the ones in the book you brought, Ileana. He must have been copying them."

Thantos began to applaud; his hands clapped loudly, keeping up a slow, steady beat. "I commend your vivid imagination, Apolla." He bowed his head, feigning respect. "It has been said that imagination is more important than knowledge. Apparently, you agree." Before Cam could protest, he hurriedly continued, "And you are to be praised for the loyalty to your guardian Karsh — misguided though it is. But there is no evidence here to verify your wild accusation." He gestured to the circular staircase, indicating that it was time to leave.

Cam knew this much. A copy of Karsh's real journal had been forged. That's what she'd seen.

For a moment, Thantos stared malevolently at Cam. A chill ran through her as she realized he could be conjuring a spell. One capable of anything from paralyzing her to transmutating her into a separate creature.

Instead, he turned, disgusted, and started up the stairs.

Ileana charged after him, grabbing his black cloak. "You did it. You had another book made, a near duplicate of Lord Karsh's sacred journal!"

Thantos turned slowly, tearing his cape from her hand. He was close to the top of the stairs. From this vantage point he glared down at Ileana. "Don't ever touch me again," he hissed menacingly, "nor cast doubt on my word in front of Miranda. Never, do you hear me?"

"Do what you will. I won't back down. That boy Cam saw, fledgling or prisoner, servant or hostage, worked under your command — under your orders to create a duplicate book and to twist its conclusion to your own advantage!"

A few steps below, Miranda and Cam stood shivering at Thantos's threat and Ileana's audacity. Cam felt it first. A sudden but soft balmy breeze enveloped them, swirling as though to wrap them in a cocoon of warmth.

Miranda gasped. Her eyes searched the narrow alley in which she and Cam stood. Above them, Thantos and Ileana were at each other, but the invisible bandage of heat encircling Cam and her mother seemed to form a protective barrier between them and the father-and-daughter face-off.

"Aron?" Miranda whispered, as if she expected a reply. Cam felt it, too. Someone or something was protecting them. A moment later she knew why.

Still holding Cam, Miranda announced, "I believe her." Her tone of quiet authority silenced the din above them. "If Cam said she saw a man, a warlock writing down here, copying Lord Karsh's handwriting, then she did. She is my daughter. And Aron's daughter — as powerful, good, and honest as her father. Born to learn and lead. She doesn't imagine things. And she doesn't lie."

"Yes!" Ileana shouted triumphantly.

Thantos spun on his heels and faced his daughter. Assuming he would try to grab the book she held, Ileana turned, intending to toss it to Miranda for safekeeping. But it wasn't Karsh's journal he was after. He caught her face between his huge hands and forced her head around, forced her to face him.

She tried to look away, but too late. Thantos's glistening black eyes bored into hers. A second later, Ileana wailed in anguish. "No. No! I'm blind. I can't see anything!"

Breaking the warm bond that joined them, Miranda pushed away from Cam. Her hand flew to her neck. Aghast, she screamed, "How could you? Thantos, you —" She never finished the sentence. With a wave of his hand, he silenced and then paralyzed her.

Cam would not be stealthed. She grasped her sun necklace and whispered as her mother had, "Aron. Father . . ." She felt the heat encasing her body center itself in the charm her father had made for her. She felt ready.

But crafty Thantos would not be predicted. He didn't seem interested in wasting or immobilizing her. "Come with me now, Apolla." He turned his back on her and walked up the few remaining stairs to his old room. "Your mother is safe. She feels no pain. You may return to her in a moment."

Cam felt safe — and curious. Clinging to her amulet, she followed him. He stopped before the low, opened hatch that had hidden the cellar.

"Only trust me, Apolla; stand with me," he said with frightening tenderness. "What does it matter which book the old warlock wrote? He is dead. I am the head of this family. When your mother marries me, *you* will inherit all this —"

Understanding came in waves, sickening but crystal clear, washing away all doubt. Of course Ileana had the true book, the book that said Aron's twins were to head the powerful DuBaer dynasty.

Of course Thantos could not tolerate that reality. Thantos, whose only true belief was in his superiority, his unearned but inalienable right to rule.

Her uncle, it was clear from everything Cam had seen, not only by his actions, but in his childhood room, had been consumed by jealousy all his life. And had tried to take what was not his through deceit, dark magick, and worse.

Cam clamped her sun charm tightly. But there was nothing he could do — he had tried and been thwarted time and again — to capture and destroy her sister and herself. None of his brutal plots had succeeded. And they never would. Not while she and Alex had each other's backs. And not with Miranda — and their guardian, Ileana — on their side. Not after their initiation.

You will never be initiated!

Whether Thantos had meant for Cam to read his mind or hadn't believed she could, Cam realized that her uncle's startling thought was also a vow. It was a promise that he intended to keep at any cost. Which was when she realized, maybe for the first time since she and Alex had met, how important it was for them to be initiated. To be empowered as full-fledged witches on their sixteenth birthday — which was only months away. To take their place in the Coventry community — and at Crailmore.

Thantos ducked and was about to leave the stairway and enter his room. "Release my mother," Cam demanded, "my mother and Ileana —"

He paused. "All in good time. Miranda is fine. She feels nothing, no pain. Do you honestly think I would harm her?"

"Why wouldn't you? You don't love her, you need her. And you didn't rescue me from the quicksand because you loved me. You needed me to get to her," Cam answered.

"Oh, but that's where you're wrong," her uncle said coldly. "I do love Miranda. I've always loved her. But she chose unwisely when she chose my brother. Aron was weak. His aims and ambitions were insane, destructive. He wanted to put all the wealth and power of the glorious DuBaer line at the service of strangers. No, I am the only one strong and determined enough to hold on to what is rightfully ours. As for you? Your mother was right. You are a powerful witch, Apolla. An alliance will benefit both of us."

Correction. An alliance with either of them, Cam or Alex, was what he needed. As long as they were kept separated, prevented from working together, their powers would be diminished, giving Thantos the upper hand. But why had he chosen her? Had she been so much easier to play?

"I admire your self-awareness," the tracker said acidly.

Good call. She could be self-aware. Beware the fool who got in her way when she did become aware of her inner slayer — and acted on it. Cam went to pin him with her eyes, but he deftly averted her heat-bearing stare.

"You're a smart girl — in a staring contest you won't win. So join me. All this will be yours. You don't need Alex. You're the star."

The star. Right.

"Where does your daughter, Ileana, fit into your grand scheme?" Cam wanted to know, but also wanted to bait him.

"She doesn't," Thantos retorted, glancing back at Ileana, who had sunk to her knees, her hands covering her blind eyes. "The mother was Antayus. The daughter is too much of a risk, a potential danger to me."

It was the way he said it. His casual honesty was chilling. He would kill Ileana and think nothing of it. And if one of Miranda's daughters had to be sacrificed for Cause DuBaer, so be it. Was he actually psychotic enough to think Miranda would be okay with that? Or that he could hide the sick truth from her forever?

Thantos's back was to her. Crouching slightly, he disappeared through the door at the top of the stairs.

"How long did you think it would be before my mother saw right through you?" Cam called after him. "All the way to your rotten core?"

"What an interesting question, coming from you," he retorted. "I should think you'd already know the answer."

Cam hurried after him. "What are you talking about?" she demanded, entering her uncle's childhood room.

"Love is blind," he said, chuckling maliciously. She

followed his gaze to a tall, strapping young warlock who stood staring out the window. "Even for the sun princess." Thantos snapped his fingers, and the boy turned.

The last thing Cam saw before she was plunged into darkness was the glint of a horseshoe pendant — the symbol, she now realized, of a Thantos loyalist. It was Shane's.

CHAPTER NINETEEN
THE BATTLE

The Traveler spell, fueled by the rage of three Furies and one ticked-off T*Witch, kicked into warp speed. At least that was how it felt to Alex, who was so winded she was practically wheezing when the spell deposited her with a jolt at the front gates of Crailmore. Her traveling companions suffered no such whiplash. All passion and purpose, they barged through the estate's massive doors, easily overpowering the few fledgling servants foolhardy enough to try to block their way.

Alex heard the voices first. Thantos was growling, "It seems we have *more* company — unexpected, unwelcome, and extremely inconvenient."

"I didn't know anything about it," Shane declared nervously. "You've got to believe me!"

Alex raced toward the tense tête-à-tête in the east wing of the mansion, where the childhood lair of America's least wanted was located.

Sersee, however, went where she had seen Thantos last and where his scent was still strong. Out of habit, Epie and Michaelina followed her down the portrait-lined corridor to the salon.

Alex burst into the tower room, ready to face her brutish uncle and his backstabbing underling. It was Cam's face that unhinged her. Her double was unfocused . . . sightless.

Thantos, of course, was ready for Alex. Stroking his dark beard, he flashed her an acidly amused look and announced, "You've come a long way. For nothing. Your sister is beyond your help. Why not leave while you're still mobile?"

"Cam!" Alex shouted, ignoring him. Holding her moon charm, she whirled on Shane. He was shaking; but she couldn't tell whether with fear or rage. "What have you done to my sister?!"

"He has blinded her with love," Thantos mocked, trying to lock eyes with Alex.

"Don't look at him," Cam frantically ordered. "Don't look at either of them." From the moment she had gazed at

Shane, Cam's precious eyesight had been damaged. The warlock and his horseshoe amulet had been burned into her retinas, blocking clear sight of anything else. Explosions of light surrounded the two images, painfully obscuring all else. "Run! Get out of here!" Cam told her sister.

It took a second for Alex to read what Cam had left unsaid — that she was almost as blind as Ileana. And another second for Alex to "see" their guardian kneeling in the dark . . . beside their mother, Miranda —

Had she really seen them? Alex's ace in the hole had always been her hyperhearing. Reading people's minds was no biggie. But seeing? To actually envision Ileana in her wretched condition, bowed and wailing in some dark cave, while Miranda was frozen in grief? Could Alex now see what Cam could not?

It's the island, her sister answered. *Being here enhances our powers*.

"Sad but true," their uncle confirmed. And Alex knew instantly that on Coventry his dark skills were strengthened, too.

Still clutching her moon amulet, which was heating up quickly, Alex turned toward the grinning trickster — exactly as he had wanted her to. But one glimpse of the firelight dancing in his black eyes, and the malevolent glint revealed his true intention. To burn her eyes, blind her as he had her sister and Ileana.

She turned away quickly, suffering a stinging pin-prick of pain. Tears momentarily blurred her vision. But as her eyes closed, her hearing became more intense than it had ever been.

Stand up, Ileana! Alex heard Miranda's far-off command. *I can see, even if I cannot move or speak. Only listen carefully to my mind and I will guide you up the stairs.*

They were in a cave; that much Alex knew. But where? Was it the cave in which the Furies had lived, under LunaSoleil?

"What shall we do with the moon child?" Thantos's deep voice called Alex's thoughts back to the tower room and the trouble she was facing. A slow, steady heat seemed to be building in the pocket of her camouflage jacket. Karsh's crystal! The pink stone had been used many times by the beloved warlock and once or twice by Alex and Cam, to help create powerful magick. Perhaps it could free Cam of their uncle's spell —

"Warlock, I am speaking to you! What shall we do?" Thantos repeated.

"Whatever you wish," Shane pledged.

Cam took hold of her sun charm and twisted her face toward Shane's voice. "Leave her alone, Shane. You may be a liar but you're not an idiot. Don't you know that what he'll do to you — whether or not you follow his commands — will be a hundred times worse than anything you can do to Alex?"

"How touching," Thantos responded. "She still loves you."

"Yes, I do," Cam called out, to Alex's horror. "I was taught — *we* were taught," her sister amended pointedly, "that vengeance hurts the revenge-seeker more than its victim. That payback is poison and that only love —"

"Conquers hate," Alex finished Cam's thought, understanding now what her sister meant — and remembering with almost painful tenderness the old tracker who had taught and given them so much. Including the pink quartz crystal in her pocket.

Thantos's booming laughter echoed in the stone-walled room. "Let's see, Shane, what would be a fitting end to your bedazzled girlfriend's twin? She is . . . a thorn in my side — yes! Shall we have thorns erupting from her skin?"

Alex watched Shane. Visibly trembling, the blond boy stood before Thantos with his head bowed. "Is that what you want?" he asked, his voice breaking nervously.

Thantos heard the hesitation. "Does that frighten you?" Driven by his instinct to attack wherever he sensed weakness, the tracker turned on his servant.

Shane fell to his knees at Thantos's feet.

"Get up, you double-dealing dog!" Sersee commanded, crashing into the room like a giant bowling ball, with tiny Michaelina at her heels.

Thantos's sneer turned to an astonished O. He'd known that Shane and Cam had put a prideful curse on Sersee, but even he was astonished. She really did resemble a prideful balloon.

Alex used the Furies' entrance to rush to Cam. The sight of Alex, though shadowy and haloed by starbursts, loosed a torrent of tears in Cam — welcome tears that bathed and soothed her wounded eyes.

"Hang on to your charm," Alex whispered. "And give me your other hand."

"You've got a plan!" Cam said softly, already beginning to smile.

"Well," Alex hedged, "I've got a crystal. It's a start. Got any incantations up your sleeve?"

"You!" Thantos growled at Sersee, regaining his composure. "You have failed me bitterly! Artemis is *here*. Here to subvert all that I have worked for! Is this how you do my bidding?"

"Why don't you ask Epie?" Sersee snapped back. "I'm alive and here, too — though you sent her to kill me. Obviously, she kinda blew it, too, wouldn't you say?" Turning back to Shane, she repeated her command. "On your feet, traitor. Undo this spell at once or I will crush you!"

The young warlock stood. His lips twitched and his jaw muscles rippled as he struggled to hide a smile. "I'm sure you could," he agreed cruelly.

Sersee's hands flew up, curved into eager claws.

"Universe of love and light, please restore my sister's sight," Alex whispered.

"Let us live to do good works —" Cam stopped, at a loss suddenly.

"And?" her twin restlessly prompted. Cam shrugged apologetically.

"Okay, okay." Alex tried to think. "Works, perks, smirks . . . Got it," she hissed triumphantly. *"And kick the butts of these betraying jerks!"*

Cam blinked — instantly, she could see, as clearly and crisply as ever.

With a whoosh, Sersee's bloated body deflated.

"Bonus," Alex explained to Sersee. To Cam, she sent a silent plea: *Come on. We've got to get to LunaSoleil. Miranda and Ileana are in trouble!*

"Yes." Thantos easily intercepted the message. "Do hurry. You're urgently needed *elsewhere*!"

"Did I thank you for giving me so many extraordinary powers for my mission?" Sersee mumbled at Thantos. "Allow me to demonstrate some of them — on you!"

Instantly, the tracker seized Shane and wrapped a thick arm around the startled boy's waist. He held his flunky in front of him like a shield, while Sersee — hands extended, ready to strike — tried to clear her head.

"They're not at LunaSoleil," Cam told her sister. "They're here. But Ileana's been blinded and he paralyzed Miranda —"

"Epie!" Shane shouted. Thantos's arm tightened against his ribs, knocking the wind out of him and cutting off anything else he might have said.

But Michaelina took up where Shane had left off. "Sers," she cried, pointing. "It's Epie!"

Thantos flashed a dangerous look Michaelina's way — then turned back to Sersee. "I should be insulted," he told her, his face distorted with barely contained rage, "that you would try such a weary trick on me. Your former associate would not dare show her face here after failing me so miserably! I'm disappointed at your lack of imagination!"

Sersee thrust her hands forward. Her fingers were slim again but every bit as competent as they'd been in Salem Woods. "You are so toast!" she shouted as fire flew from her hands. Still gripping his hostage, Thantos sidestepped the blaze, while Shane tried desperately to wriggle out of Sersee's way. The blazing bolt missed him, but random sparks scorched his shirt — revealing the horseshoe pendant underneath. Sersee laughed gleefully and aimed her fiery eyes at the charm. It spun rapidly, tightening the chain around Shane's neck. When it stopped, the horseshoe hung upside down — a sign of bad fortune.

"There! It's turned," Sersee gloated. "And so has your luck! Get out of my way, you two-faced fool, before I fry both your faces." The rabid witch screamed at Shane, "I'll deal with you later. Now it's the great Lord Liar's turn."

Thantos shoved Shane out of the way. "Take your best shot, impudent guttersnipe!" he railed at Sersee.

Sersee shoved her hands forward, her palms facing his heart. A great tongue of fire leaped forward.

With a seemingly effortless exhalation, Thantos blew it back, sent it curling in on the witch. It licked at the hood of her cloak and set her raven hair aflame, filling the room with a crackling sulfur stench.

The tracker's victorious smile faded as Epie rushed to her old colleague and, tossing her own cape over Sersee's head, smothered the blaze.

"You!" Thantos cried. With a glowering glance, he flattened the girl. Epie crumpled to the floor. The cloak — which had completed its task — flew up from her arms, then drifted down over her.

"She's not alone!" Mike had found her voice again.

Ileana, still blinded, was standing unsteadily before the low hatch to the underground chamber. Alex and Cam had never seen her so vulnerable before. They ran to her but before they could recite the incantation that had reversed Cam's blindness, Ileana put her hands on Cam's shoulder and urged, "Use the coin. Now! The DuBaer medallion!"

"Where's Miranda?" Alex asked their guardian as Cam searched her pockets for the gold disk inscribed with the crowned bear.

"Your mother is in the caves below."

"I'm going to get her," Alex declared as Cam fished frantically for the coin. Had she left it in Aron's room? What had she been wearing the morning Ileana slipped her the medallion?

"No." Ileana laid a hand on Alex's shoulder. "She can't move, but her mind and sight and ability to communicate telepathically are whole. She is safe for now —"

Thantos reached into his herb pouch and pulled out a handful of fragrant dried leaves.

"Watch out!" Michaelina hollered. She'd been standing between Ileana and Thantos. Now she ducked desperately.

Sersee, who had been taunting Shane, keeping him on his knees by hurling fire at him, looked up.

"Camryn," the tracker boomed, hiding the herbs in his fist, "you have one final chance. I offer it for the sake of the woman I love —"

"Excuse me?" Ileana was flabbergasted. "Would that be the same woman you turned into stone?"

As always, her father ignored her. "Trust me, Cam," he continued, "and become my ally —"

Cam was so bowled over by the man's gall, she almost lost it. "Your ally? Trust you? Let me think about this. . . ." She took a deep breath. It was crucial to stay calm, keep her voice level, critical to keep her opponent off balance. "On the one hand, you did promise that if I helped you, we could be the most powerful family Coventry had ever seen. You, Miranda, and me, just the three of us."

Stunned, Alex swung her head between her sister — "He did?" — and her uncle. "You did?"

"Well, yeah." Cam had walked up to her uncle, nearly got in Thantos's face, but then faked to the left — forcing him to twist around to see her — before settling on his right side. To Alex, she said evenly, "Our beloved uncle said you were dispensable. He pretty much erased you from the family portrait."

Alex's eyes widened. She could practically feel the word *Fool* being etched on her forehead. She'd almost fallen for it! She'd even told Cade she was leaving — because "Sara" had told her to go. Alex would have done anything she truly believed to be her late mom's wishes.

Score! That's exactly what Thantos had banked on. But the big guy, the mastermind, had miscalculated. He didn't know Sara. How could he ever have understood a woman whose heart was full of love, when his own boiled with jealousy and hate? Which led Alex to wonder out loud, "What if I didn't do what Sara's spirit told me to? What if I didn't leave?"

"My guess?" Cam said, again careful to keep emotion out of her voice. "If not west, you'd go south. As in, six feet under. No Alex? No sweat."

"After all," Ileana put in through gritted teeth, "it's easy to kick a child to the curb. Who'd know better than the Father of the Year here?"

Thantos's eyes hardened, but he remained silent.

"Okay, wait," Cam said slowly, convincingly. She gifted Thantos with her most sincere look. "I was raised to be fair, so before I condemn him, let me be sure I understand. Alex and Ileana are gone, and while we're at it, I guess I say buh-bye to Dave, Emily, Dylan, my friends in Marble Bay. So it'll be all me, all Coventry, all the time. That about right?"

Thantos nodded carefully.

She paused, let her gaze slide to the window. "There

are worse places to be. Who knows? Maybe I could learn to feel a part of it, to love it even."

A muffled sound rose from the floor. "Don't trust him!"

Cam focused on the round mound at her feet. She'd almost forgotten poor Epie, trapped under the cape. She made no move to help the hapless Fury, only noted, "I am his niece, Epie. It might be okay for me to trust him. At least give him a chance to earn my trust."

Alex started to speak, but Ileana knew enough to stay quiet and to telepathically warn her charge to do the same. The moment of reckoning had come, and to her credit, Camryn was not telegraphing her real intentions or feelings. Aron's sun princess daughter was playing this close to the vest, playing it out. Ileana could only hope she'd do the right thing.

Cam continued thoughtfully, "In another year or so, my life as I've known it is going to change, anyway. My friends will all be gone, off to college — and I guess I will be, too. So why not come here? I could get used to living in the lap of luxury, either here at Crailmore, or more likely, at LunaSoleil, where I was meant to grow up. Be with my real mother, among my blood relations."

Michaelina couldn't hold back. "Are you a bigger dupe than your sister?"

Cam whirled on the short, stupefied Fury. "Hang on,

Mike. Put yourself in my Manolos. If I stay here, I've got money, power, popularity, fame. Think of all the good I could do, the position I'd be in to really help the world's people. And, ooooh, bonus! I've got Shane." She gazed at him, cowering on the floor, trying to fend off Sersee's fiery blows. "Coventry's best catch," Cam added, struggling to keep the sarcasm out of her voice.

Sersee growled, "I wouldn't bet on any of that."

Cam rolled her eyes. "Puh-leeze, Sersee, as if you ever posed any threat to me. Like you said, I am an heiress."

Thantos blinked — uncertain now.

Cam circled him. "Kudos, Uncle Thantos. You really know me well, after all. My loyalty can be bought — the currency being my superficiality, my superiority complex, my absolute comfort in life at the top. Like niece, like uncle, that's what you figured, right?"

Alex was totally stunned. Not at her sister — at Thantos! He was lapping this garbage right up! Quickly, Alex scrambled her thoughts, so he wouldn't hear her.

He didn't. Too engrossed in the possibility he'd get all he wanted after all, close enough to almost taste victory, Thantos ventured, "DuBaer blood runs through you, Apolla. Untainted DuBaer blood. You are heir to much more than you ever dreamed possible. Make the right choice, Apolla. It's what your father would have wanted for you."

He'd almost done it. Mentioning Aron would have been the one thing to set her off, but Cam would not play. She'd gotten this far; her real feelings weren't getting out of the box now. She dug into her pocket, and then quietly, evenly, she said, "My father would have wanted me to trust you. Yes? Well, in that case . . ."

She fell to her knees, bowed her head in a worshipful pose. She could sense, rather than see, the grin forming on her uncle's vicious face. He reached for her, to take her hand.

She extended her right hand, "I guess I could give you the chance, try and trust you." In the split second before they actually touched, sealed the deal, Cam sprang up out of his reach. "On the other hand? Nah. Think I'll bust you instead."

Buried deep inside her pocket, she'd found the amulet, the DuBaer family heirloom that Ileana had given her. Alex was by her side in a flash.

Thantos's jaw set dangerously. He acted swiftly, but again, unpredictably. He did not go for the amulet, and try to harm Cam, Alex, or even Ileana. His first act was to level the battlefield. The dried leaves he'd fisted were fragrant and powerful herbs, used to confuse and disorient those forced to inhale them. Thantos opened his palm and blew on the leaves, sending airborne flakes toward the Furies. In midair, the dried leaves fused together and formed rings, curlicues that found their victims, coiled around them like a lariat, and pulled the three together tightly. They looked like three unwilling participants in a three-legged race, one limb from each practically fused to that of her friend. One move, together or separately, and their unwieldiness would bring them down. Just in case they tried, however, Thantos made sure searing pain would result. His chant boomed like thunder:

> *Every day has its dawn, and every rose its*
> *thorn —*
> *Every dawn is dusk, every Fury her trust.*
> *Wayward witches three, like wildflowers may*
> *you be, sticking together, pricking one*
> *another as you twist and turn in the*
> *wind.*

Even as he cast the spell, sharp thorns poked through Sersee's skinny arms, Michaelina's diminutive legs, and Epie's chubby hands. The Furies broke into an instant shrieking chorus of "ouch!" And "get away from me!"

The combination of pricking pain, petulance, and

being ticked off rendered the Furies neutralized. A non-threat.

By immobilizing the turncoat Furies, Thantos had eliminated three enemies. But he'd also wasted valuable seconds giving the T*Witches a golden chance to advance on him. They snapped to it.

Cam held the DuBaer family amulet high. It would act as a protective shield against the terrible power of their uncle. Forcing him to hesitate, at least for a moment, they worked double-strength magick on him. Powers that previously had been the domain of only one of them worked in tandem. Two pairs of extraordinary gray eyes now stunned and pinned Thantos, froze the giant warlock to the spot, his mouth locked in an O, his beady eyes stuck in shock-reaction. Telekinesis-times-two double-knotted his hands behind his back with the velvet rope from his own robe. He couldn't move, couldn't speak, and couldn't strike them. Cam wanted to make sure he could see what was happening. She lined up the mirrors in the room so all Thantos could see, over and over again, was his own paralyzed image.

"We did it! Ileana!" Alex raced over to her still-blinded guardian. "Wait until we lift this spell, you'll see! He can't hurt us now."

Cam caught a flash of indigo. Blue-robed Shane had

witnessed a dose of double DuBaer and made his decision. He was outta there! "Not so fast," Cam growled, advancing on him. "I'm not finished with you! We'll help Ileana, and then it will be my pleasure to deal with you."

"You'll do neither," Ileana said forcefully, her unfocused eyes burning brightly. "Your mother is your priority. Let the coward flee, and leave me be. Miranda's already waited too long. Go to her."

"But it'll just take a minute —" Alex started, unable to stand by while Ileana remained sightless.

"What if he hurts you?" Cam meant Shane, but the boy had already sprinted toward the door.

"As long as I am your guardian, you'll do as I say. Leave me, get Miranda!"

CHAPTER TWENTY
MIRANDA'S GAME

Cam led Alex through the door-hatch, and together they scrambled down the dark tunnel. Alex marveled at Cam's agility, how her twin so swiftly and economically negotiated her way down the narrow twisty stairs, while calling out to Miranda. This is what Cam had been dealing with while Alex had been — what? Letting Michaelina take her for a fool? Pouring her wounded heart out to Sersee, disguised as Sara?

And don't forget your friend, the dark-haired boy, and the hours you spent with or wanting him.

Alex's eyes widened. Through the gloom she saw Miranda, frozen in place. But how could their mother have known . . . standing there now, her white robes draped stiffly as a Greek statue's?

My body may be immobilized, but my mind is as active as ever. More so, came the reply. *The powers I thought were gone forever have been reawakened more quickly than I'd hoped. I'm your mother. And fate has seen fit to return the most precious of all my lost gifts — the ability to know my children; know their minds and hearts — and, yes, even their whereabouts.*

"Close your mouth," Cam advised her sister, whose jaw had dropped. "Let's do this thing. There'll be plenty of time for Mom to rag on you later and out loud."

The twins sandwiched Miranda, linking their arms around her slender waist. It was almost as if the warmth of their touch melted Miranda's frozen body, but more likely, it was the right combination of herbs, that crystal of Alex's, their moon and sun necklaces working together, and the unbreakable bond of love between mother and children.

Once Miranda was free, the threesome wasted no time: catch-up could come later. Ileana had waited long enough. She needed them now. Jubilantly, they raced up the stairs. But their joy faded with the sight that greeted them back in Thantos's room.

Thantos was no longer captive. No ropes bound his wrists together. He glared menacingly at the sight of

Camryn and Alex, their arms protectively wrapped around their mother's waist.

How Thantos had gotten free of their spell was a no-brainer. He'd borrowed the brains of others — not only had Shane returned, the stupidly loyal boy had brought backup: Amaryllis. Thantos's servant had been imbued with extra powers, along with the mission to spy on Cam. With Shane, she'd been able to undo the T*Witches' spell.

Two times three: The trios faced one another. Shane, Amaryllis, and Thantos on one side, Miranda and her twins on the other. In the middle of the battlefield? The untethered Ileana, sightless, and for now, speechless. A hostage, should Thantos so decree, Alex realized immediately.

Don't worry about me! Ileana shouted telepathically. *Get them!*

Miranda acted so quickly and unexpectedly, she threw the entire room off balance. She freed herself of Cam and Alex, shooed them from her side.

A step toward Thantos was deliberate and risky. She looked kindly at him. "May I speak to you now? I have my voice back, as you can see, and with it, my reasoning."

Thantos's thin lips pressed together to form a straight line. Almost imperceptibly he nodded at Miranda. He took in, Cam could see with horror, her mother's diaphanous beauty, her pale skin, her pure heart. His own icy countenance *could* be melted.

"If you would call off your dogs for one moment, we would all be best served," Miranda said.

"What is it you want to talk about, Miranda?" Thantos asked, his voice a combination of hope and fury.

"The things I've only just found out. You never told me your true feelings for me. My daughters only just did. This changes everything."

His eyes were so hard to read! Alex tapped into Cam's brain — could she see what was inside those mirrors to her uncle's soul? But Cam was mute, either shocked into silence or quiet by calculation. Alex knew only to trust her.

"It isn't too late, Thantos," Miranda was murmuring. "You haven't done irreparable damage yet. Let us forget the past and focus on now. And our future. I won't hoodwink you. I don't love you — not yet. But I am a fair woman, you have always known me to be so. I offer you this: Come, let me hear your side of everything."

Thantos stood rock still. He did not give away his emotions.

Miranda continued as if he'd made up his mind, "But first, you must free your daughter of the hateful curse she's under and unglue these three girls. We will send them away, Sersee, Epie, and Michaelina, as well as your loyalists, Amaryllis and Shane. This is neither their battle nor their business. This is a family matter. Our family."

Miranda said it sweetly and sternly, a woman in such control, at this point, not even her daughters knew how sincere she really was. Her mission was accomplished, though: Thantos was willing to chance it.

Miranda assured him, "I will ensure that Ileana and my daughters do not interfere with our talk. You have my word. Do I have yours?"

No one had to break into the great tracker's skull to know what was going through it. Maybe he really did love her. His body language gave it away. He was on the brink of allowing himself to be led.

Miranda gently coaxed him forward. "Will you do that, Thantos? Will you trust me?"

Still, he made no move, until Miranda came out with it. "If you don't trust me, you can't possibly love me."

It was done practically before she got the words out. Ileana was finally restored of her sight and her faculties. The Furies were dethorned, unglued, and sent packing — Shane and Amaryllis left, too.

Miranda allowed herself a wide smile. It dazzled Thantos. She took his hand. "Come, let's have some privacy. We'll talk next door."

Aron's room. She was leading her vile brother-in-law into the childhood room of her husband, where his spirit, his magick, could be keenly felt. But Thantos was too far gone to resist. He was like putty!

Miranda turned to her daughters and her niece. "I'm asking you to stay put. Do not follow us, and please, do not eavesdrop. You must not."

Cam was nervous, unwilling to capitulate to Miranda's request. Alex shared the concern that Thantos could still hurt her. It was Ileana who found her inner rationale, her calm, and her trust. "Your mother has to make up her mind on her own. It's in her hands now. And whatever decision she makes is the one we'll all have to abide by."

Miranda led Thantos through the door — and closed it.

"Okay, then, we won't eavesdrop," Cam agreed. "But we don't have to shut off our senses, either."

"Excellent." Alex high-fived her, while Ileana shrugged her consent.

"What do you see?" Alex pressed her sister.

Cam closed her eyes and opened her mind "Ugh," she grunted as the foggy image began to grow crisp. "She just sat down on that little couch —"

"The divan," Ileana informed her.

"And she's patting the place next to her, inviting him to sit beside her."

Alex tensed. The deceitful trickster was too close

for comfort. Like her sister, using her inner senses, she strained to hear what was being said.

Miranda's voice was softly soothing. "I've known you since you were a child, Thantos. And though I've admitted that my feelings are unclear, I can tell you how your brother felt: He loved you. Unconditionally. You were his blood."

Alex rolled her eyes. Her mother was playing the big heel. She could hear it — and so, she realized with awe, could Cam. Her sister's mojo was on Miracle-Gro! And Cam was smiling smugly, thinking exuberantly, *How cool is our mom?*

Thantos was so not. Like a stammering teenager, he urged, "Then you believe that Aron would want us to be together? To have a family of our own, to have a son."

"Let's ask him," their mother proposed. "My powers are too diminished, but will you call up Aron's spirit, Thantos? Let us find out what he would have wished."

There was a pause. Despite herself, Ileana strained forward.

"What's happening?" Alex asked.

Cam shut her eyes again. "He's freaking," she said.

Suddenly, Alex could see it, too. Hazily, to be sure, but she could see her mother and the tracker facing each other on the . . . divan . . . and that the color had drained from their uncle's ruddy face. "No," he was pleading, "it's too dangerous. I mean, I don't think it's wise. Because — let us settle this together, between ourselves, without disturbing poor Aron's restless spirit —"

Ileana gasped. When Cam and Alex looked at her, she whispered, "He's afraid of your father! Afraid of what your father will say! Miranda has won the game. He can't have her without Aron's permission and he is too fearful to ask for it."

"Yesss!" Alex cheered, beginning to giggle. Cam and Ileana looked at each other and nearly choked. It took all their self-control not to laugh and snort like children.

"He is so done," Cam reported. "Look at him, he looks more deflated than Sersee —"

"The bigger they are, the harder they fall," was Alex's gleeful opinion.

"He can't even look at her!" Ileana reported, too intrigued with what she was seeing to realize that yet another of her lost powers had returned. "She's waiting —"

"But he's got nothing to say," Cam whispered.

"Shhh, they're getting up." Alex heard the rustling, saw the misty figures standing. Miranda, tall and regal; Thantos checkmated by the queen.

By the time Miranda reentered the room, her daughters had plunked themselves onto Thantos's bed and were raptly listening to Ileana as she drilled them on spell-casting.

The man who followed their mother was a shell. Head bowed, massive shoulders hunched dejectedly, he was running on empty. No ropes bound him; no blows had knocked him over. Miranda's wit had triumphed over Thantos's iron will.

He glanced at them as if disinterested. "If you will excuse me," he murmured, hurrying past them, making his way to the door.

"You were brilliant!" Ileana hurried to hug Miranda. Alex followed close on her guardian's sandaled heels.

"Way to go, Mom." Cam joined the huddle.

Miranda embraced them enthusiastically, realizing with gratitude that she alone had read her brother-in-law's parting thought as he'd looked at her children. *This is not over!* he'd warned.

CHAPTER TWENTY-ONE
PLAYING TO WIN

Cam closed her eyes, tilted her face upward to let the sun caress it. "Sun-kissed." She'd always loved being described that way. She smiled.

Next to her, Alex sat cross-legged, leaning back, palms pressed against the warm wooden pier. She listened to the music of gentle waves lapping the sandy shore.

The twins were back in Marble Bay. They were waiting for Dave and Emily's cruise ship to return to the dock. And they were doing some serious thinking.

The summer had blasted off with Fourth of July fireworks and continued apace, one emotional explosion, one terrifying blast after another. Cam had almost lost her life; Alex, her faith in herself.

Now, less than two weeks later, the T*Witches were ready for some downtime. Some peace.

A breeze lifted strands of Cam's auburn hair out of the banana-yellow scrunchie holding it back in a pony-tail. Alex ran her fingers through her own unevenly clipped 'do and sniffed the sweet, salty air.

The tension was only slowly leaving their bodies: Cam envisioned the sensation like thick, syrupy liquid draining from them, slipping through the slats of the dock. She willed the ocean to take it out with the tide.

Both knew — it didn't need to be said — that the weeks ahead, the rest of the summer, would be the calm before the storm. Their initiation as full-fledged witches was scheduled for the fall, around the time of their six-teenth birthday. And there was nothing they could do to stop that from happening. Initiation was the starting point, the opening gate, the first step on the road that would lead to their destiny. The path ahead was theirs to walk. They could only vow to walk it together.

Back in Coventry, after Miranda had disabled Thantos, she and Ileana had taken the twins outside, where they'd walked through the fragrant herb garden Miranda had been nurturing lovingly. There, the women finally told the girls all they needed to know.

They read passages from the book, the true book Karsh Antayus had written and bequeathed to Ileana. In order for Cam and Alex to understand what lay in store for them, what their grandfather's wishes had been, they had to understand their family's history.

Cam had marveled, her heart swelling with pride, and just as often, withering with disappointment, as she listened to tales of heroism and betrayal, spells of love and curses of doom, conjured up and carried out by those in her own DNA pool.

Alex could practically hear the tape rewind. All she'd ever been taught about the Salem witch trials — history books and fiction classics like *The Crucible*, replayed in front of her eyes. Only now the characters in the novels were her own kin.

The twins had learned about the curse that haunted their family: Because Jacob DuBaer had exposed Abigail Antayus as a witch, she'd been hanged. Her children had cursed the DuBaer family. In each generation, an Antayus would kill a DuBaer.

Cam and Alex had been shocked when Miranda and Ileana — reading Karsh's words — confirmed that the curse was real. That it had never skipped a generation. That even when their grandfather Nathaniel DuBaer and Karsh Antayus had become best of friends, had pledged to end it in their lifetimes, the curse had prevailed. It had proved stronger, more powerful than the great will and pure hearts of these good men. It had been a heinous, horrible accident — absolutely — but in the end, Thantos had been right about one thing: Karsh had caused the death of Nathaniel.

The curse, though, had one qualification: It applied only to males. The dying wish, then, of their grandfather was, as Ileana had read: *"From this time forth, only women shall rule the DuBaer dynasty, only women shall head the family."* And then the curse would be no more.

Of course, Ileana had explained, Thantos knew of his father's decision — the pact that would rob him of his right to rule the powerful and rich family. The bitter tracker's jealousy of Aron had started the day his younger brother was born — and had only grown stronger with the passing years as he watched Aron shine and grow to his most bountiful goodness. But when his brother's wife gave birth to twin girls, *female heirs,* Thantos's rage and envy turned to hatred. He vowed to see that these children would never stand in his way.

The hulking warlock's ultimate goal was simple: He wanted Cam and Alex out of his way. He didn't really care how he achieved that. He could separate them — send one away and lure the other to his side, or, failing that, kill one or both of them. He'd spent the better part of one full year plotting, scheming, using others to do his bidding, anything to remove them from his way. Anything to change destiny.

The twins had listened as, gently but firmly, their

mother and their cousin read Lord Karsh's dying words to them, then closed the leather-bound book and insisted that Alex and Cam take time to think over all they'd learned, take the rest of the summer to digest it.

Ilcana suggested that they leave Coventry and get back to Marble Bay, back to the safety, comfort, and love of Emily and David Barnes. "We need you to be rested, to be strong," she had said.

"And I need you to promise me . . ." Miranda had searched their eyes beseechingly. "That you will try to have fun, to spend the rest of the summer as carefree and untroubled as you can."

She didn't have to add that the next several weeks might be their last carefree ones for a long while.

Now, Cam and Alex sat together on this shockingly brilliant summer morning. It was several hours before the ship they'd come to meet was due to dock. They had the pier to themselves.

And their thoughts were in sync. "He played us."

They burst out laughing. They'd said it out loud at the same moment, capped off by another think-alike: "Could we have been any stupider?"

Thantos had played hard on their vulnerabilities — on Alex's need to square things with Sara, to feel independent, to prove she hadn't changed now that she was part of the Barnes family. To her, he'd sent Mike: the little witch who could bring friendship and a reminder of all Alex's dreams. And he'd offered her the biggest dream of all: to "see" Sara again.

He'd played on Cam's isolation, her mixed-up emotions for Jason, and her attraction to Shane, the alluring warlock whom Thantos had gifted with exceptional powers.

Worst of all, Thantos had played on her snobbishness, Cam thought miserably. She did like being number one — the most popular, winningest athlete; cute, coin-infused — she had a great life and loved it. The second that life was threatened — even momentarily, even just for the summer — Thantos had moved in and set his plan in motion.

Luckily, that plan had been blasted to smithereens. He'd been done in by his own pride.

"Thantos is our uncle, and he was right about one thing. Like it or not, we do share his blood. There is a part of Ileana, and certainly of me," Cam said, "that's — I don't know, vain, power-hungry. Gullible."

"And a part of me that's maybe too independent for my own good," Alex said. "Who doesn't see the big picture, acts rashly — dismisses the good guy's suspicions to fall into the clutches of the bad friend! What are you going to tell me, I've found my inner Fredo?"

That gave them both a laugh.

They shared the sharp memory of Miranda's last words before she'd packed up the twins and sent them back to Marble Bay. "We all have vulnerabilities," she'd told them. "If we didn't, we simply would not be human. Thantos played on yours and almost won. But he, too, is human. He, too, has vulnerabilities. Never forget that."

They never would. Miranda, their brilliant mother, had taken revenge on Thantos for the intolerable things he'd done to her daughters and to Ileana. She was the only one who could get back at him, for she held the key to his weakness. *She* was his vulnerability.

Cam had started a litany of "if only"s. If only she'd recognized the signs, had learned about the legends and myths, the horse and the horseshoe pendant. If only she hadn't been so needy, so —

"Human?" Alex had asked rhetorically. "Yo, in the self-flagellation battle, it's a tie for the gold. How'd I manage not to know Michaelina had been sent here to play me, to make me believe she could bring Sara back? How'd I manage not to know I wasn't seeing or talking to my mother? It didn't work only because Sersee kept putting the wrong words into Sara's mouth."

Maybe it runs in the family.

Alex and Cam exchanged quick, surprised looks. They'd both heard it. Then they burst out laughing.

They'd gotten a telepathic reminder from Miranda. Had she, too, not been duped? For years! By Thantos.

"I believed the person I shouldn't have," Alex noted, thinking of Mike, "and dismissed the one telling the truth. Worse? I dismissed my own gut. I knew Cade was a keeper, still, I didn't really listen to him . . . because," she finished regretfully, "he's not a warlock. I figured, what could he know? He knew Michaelina wasn't to be trusted. He knew something wasn't right."

"Guess he wanted what was best for you," Cam said, remembering something Dave had once told her: "That's what love is. Wanting what's best for the other person. And I think that may be more powerful than witchcraft."

"I bet I know what Karsh would say if he were here," Alex mused.

"'Give it a rest, T*Witches'?" Cam guessed. "Like, 'at the end of the day, Thantos lost again'?"

But they both knew that was only partly true. The battle had been won, but there were greater dangers ahead.

Cam turned to face the water and, in the distance, saw what no one else could. A ship, still far away, slowly approaching. It was bringing everything Miranda and Ileana had wished for them: safety, security, and stability. It was bringing Dave and Emily Barnes home.

ABOUT THE AUTHORS

H.B. Gilmour is the author of numerous best-selling books for adults and young readers, including the *Clueless* movie novelization and series; *Pretty in Pink,* a University of Iowa Best Book for Young Readers; and *Godzilla,* a Nickelodeon Kids Choice nominee. She also cowrote the award-winning screenplay *Tag.*

H.B. lives in upstate New York with her husband, John Johann, and their yellow lab, Harry, one of the family's five dogs, five cats, two snakes (a boa constrictor and a python), and five extremely bright, animal-loving children.

Randi Reisfeld has written many best-sellers, such as the *Clueless* series (which she wrote with H.B.), the *Moesha* series, and biographies of Prince William, New Kids on the Block, and Hanson. Her Scholastic paperback *Got Issues Much?* was named an ALA Best Book for Reluctant Readers in 1999.

Randi has always been fascinated with the randomness of life. . . . About how any of our lives can simply "turn on a dime" and instantly (snap!) be forever changed. About the power each one of us has deep inside, if only we knew how to access it. About how any of us would react if, out of the blue, we came face-to-face with our exact double.

From those random fascinations, T*Witches was born.

Oh, and BTW: She has no twin (that she knows of) but an extremely cool family and a cadre of bffs to whom she is totally devoted.

THE COVENTRY ISLAND ALMANAC

TABLE OF CONTENTS

THE COVENTRY ISLAND ALMANAC

INTRODUCTION

Witch Island. That's what the folks on the main-land call it. And that's why, even though it's a mere hop, skip, and puddle-jump across Lake Superior, between Michigan's upper peninsula and the north-ern shore of Wisconsin, no one ever goes there. They're too scared! But they shouldn't be.

"Coventry Island" is what natives call it, and hun-dreds of people with extraordinary powers and highly developed skills live there. Over the ages, these people have been called seers, shamans, sibyls, and oracles. Today, mostly everyone calls them witches.

Coventry witches and warlocks are dedicated to using their powers and their gifts to help anyone in need. Once upon a time, the founding families them-selves were in need. They were persecuted, kicked out, shamed, and shunned. These were people who ran for their lives.

And came to settle on Coventry Island.

HISTORY OF COVENTRY ISLAND

The Founding of Coventry Island

In the winter of 1692, a group of young girls in Salem, Massachusetts, started to behave strangely. The ignorant and prejudiced leaders of their community blamed the girls' condition on witchcraft. For almost the whole of that year, the Salem Witchcraft Trials accused and convicted many. Twenty-four accused witches died. The witch-hunts affected not only Salem, but also eight other villages in Essex County, Massachusetts, and Connecticut.

A powerful physician named Jacob DuBaer knew his own unique gifts would soon be questioned. He slipped away under cover of night, and began a long and difficult journey west.

In 1693, Jacob arrived at a deserted island hidden in the daybreak mist of Lake Superior, off the northern coast of Wisconsin. He had with him the beautiful young bride he found on his long journey, and the gray-eyed son who was born along the way. He named their new home "Coventry."

From the North, the land now known as Canada, to which their French ancestors had fled, came the descendants of Jean de la Rochelle. At the same time in history, Providence Antayus-Hazlitt arrived on the island with his wife, an acclaimed witch of mixed Afro-Caribbean and Native American heritage. Providence was one of the sons of the beloved healer Abigail Antayus, whom Jacob DuBaer had denounced as a witch in Salem, in order to turn suspicion away from himself.

Waves of settlers followed the three families. Witches and warlocks from every part of the world came seeking refuge to practice their craft. Native shamans, African Chango practitioners, Chinese herbalists, Celtic *ollamh* or doctors, rainmakers, geologists versed in the power of crystals, water dousers, and other skilled practitioners of the craft all found their way to Coventry. To freedom.

FOUNDING FAMILIES

Jacob DuBaer — Chastity Wright

Isaiah DuBaer | Joseph DuBaer | Isabel DuBaer | William DuBaer

Nathaniel DuBaer — Leila Tavisham

Fredo DuBaer — Coco Lopez

Vey DuBaer | Tsuris DuBaer

- - - - - Past generations
———— Direct descendants

OF COVENTRY

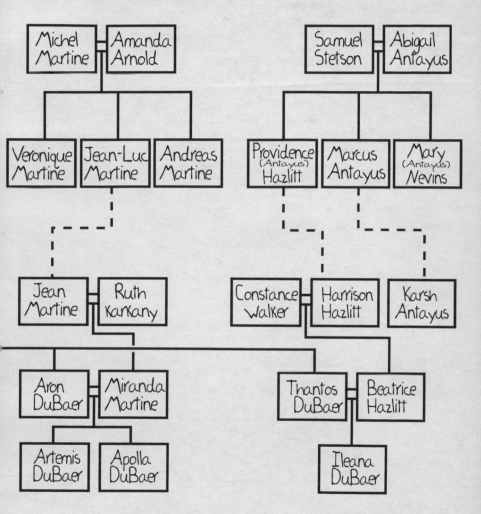

THE PROPHECY OF THE GRAY EYES

In the sixteenth century, fierce battles erupted all over Europe among opposing groups and governments — each of whom believed their way of life was the only correct one. As these wars were waged, millions of innocent people died for holding different beliefs. Among them were gifted healers and seers labeled "witches." [1] This was the bloody period that gave rise to *La Prophétie Aux Yeux Gris* — the legendary "Prophecy of the Gray Eyes."

Although they didn't know it, a few gray-eyed families living in northern France around 1550 shared a common ancestor called The First. The First was the most powerful healer of Paleolithic times, approximately 25,000–30,000 years ago. People believed her startling metallic-gray eyes were connected to her superior gifts.

By the late sixteenth century, the few families who bore these eyes—all of them healers and descendants of The First—were very distantly related and had never met. But the mysterious eyes they shared drew the notice of fearful leaders. The warmongers accused anyone possessing these eyes of witchcraft, and began to hunt and imprison them.

1. The term "witches" is sometimes used to describe both females and males gifted in the magick arts.

Mad rulers and, in many instances, ignorant populations demanded their death.

Five such witches met for the first time while in prison awaiting trial. Shocked to discover in others the eyes that had always belonged only to them, the three women and two men came to believe that their meeting was not accidental.

The night before they were all to be executed, they gathered secretly to pledge their faith to each other. Shielded by the dark of the new moon in Jupiter, they decreed a prophecy:

Let it be written that the gray-eyed descendants of The First will someday be reunited. In thirteen generations there will come a sacred marriage between a gray-eyed man and woman. The offspring of this union, whose birth on the last day of October will bridge the moment between the setting of the full moon and the rising sun, will be imbued with powers greater than those of all others, and equal to those of The First. Thus will be restored the awesome power of our kind. In this way will we be vindicated, and things set right.

Calling upon their natural gifts, the five prisoners escaped, striking out in different directions to better their chances. One of those present for the prophecy was Jacob DuBaer's grandfather, the healer Henri, who fled his native land after being accused of witchcraft. Another was Jeanne de la Rochelle, who made her way to South Africa. Sadly, the other man and two women were recaptured.

A generation later, in 1620, Henri's son, Ephram DuBaer, left his home in England, sailing on a vessel called the *Mayflower*. He needed the freedom promised in the New World to practice his arts and express his beliefs. So, like his father before him, Ephram fled the land of his birth. This is how the family DuBaer eventually came to be in America.

Ephram settled in the Plymouth Colony, where his skills as a botanist and healer brought him great wealth and renown. He had one son and six daughters by two wives. Jacob was the eldest and soon, like his father and his father before him, he gained a reputation as a great healer. Jacob, of course, would go on to found Coventry Island.

Three hundred years after the uttering of the Prophecy, two descendants of Coventry's earliest and most prominent families, Miranda Martine and Aron DuBaer, married. The stage was finally set for the fulfillment of the Prophecy of the Gray Eyes.

COVENTRY TODAY

PROMINENT PEOPLE

The Good

The citizens of Coventry Island are overwhelmingly peaceful. They are, for the most part, decent healers, and excellent neighbors. A number of people have distinguished themselves as leaders of the community:

Lady Rhianna, head of the current Unity Council, leads with the great wisdom that comes with age. She is descended from the scholarly Afro-Caribbean branch of the Adonay family and was first in her Coventry Academy Class. *Signature scents:* cocoa, coconut

Lord Grivveniss is a direct descendant of Daniell Grivviness, a Providence healer who aided Jacob DuBaer on his seventeenth-century journey toward Coventry Island. This Esteemed Elder's seminar in advanced transmutation is one of the most popular senior electives at the Initiation Academy. He will take over leadership of the Unity Council at the end of Lady Rhianna's rotation. *Signature scents:* schmaltz, paprika, and onions.

Lady Fan, former head of the Unity Council, has made invaluable contributions to the community as Curator of the History Museum. Her traveling interactive exhibit, "The Path of the Goddess: Gray Eyes in Witch History," has visited sister museums in New Orleans, Key West, and Los Angeles, where the Esteemed Elder was guest of honor at a party hosted by actor Brice Stanley. *Signature scents:* lotus, ginger, and soy.

Lord Karkum, Esteemed Elder/Unity Council, supervises the Food Co-op located at the intersection of Earth and Fire roads. He introduced the recycling program to Coventry Island. *Signature scents:* saffron, olive, and mandrake.

Lady Shiva, Esteemed Elder/Unity Council, recently retired from her position as Director of the

Public Gardens, but can still be found most after-
noons among the flowers, urging them to grow.
Signature scents: jasmine, sandalwood, and cumin.

Lady Iolande, Esteemed Elder, has just overseen
the completion of the new classroom wing at the
Airborne Arts Society, where she has managed the
flying education of Coventry's youth for more than
twenty-one years. *Signature scents:* bayberry, wiste-
ria, and heliotrope.

Lord Persiphus, Esteemed Elder, continues to serve
as Master of the Geologic Foundation, and is recognized around the world as the foremost expert on
alchemy and crystal-cleansing rituals. *Signature
scents:* talc, copper, and sulfur.

Lord Gordion, Esteemed Elder, is Chairman of the
Coventry Free Library System. Under his supervi-
sion, both the Genealogical Library and the Library
of Spells and Incantations have gone "online"
through a generous donation of the latest technology from 3 Brothers, a subsidiary of the DuBaer-owned

CompUMage empire. *Signature scents:* sage, sweet-grass, and dust.

Ileana DuBaer is guardian of the DuBaer twins. Our grateful community will never forget her loyalty and bravery on behalf of Lord Karsh — up to even the moment of his death. *Signature scents:* honey, thyme, and Chanel No. 5.

Miranda DuBaer, widow of the greatly missed Aron DuBaer, has recently returned, after an extended illness, to Coventry Island, where she's been reunited with her long-lost daughters. *Signature scents:* pine, lavender, and rosemary.

Artemis ("Alex Fielding") and **Apolla ("Camryn Barnes") DuBaer.** These twins have become a great source of curiosity and excitement for the locals during their occasional visits. Any child of DuBaer-Martine lineage would be destined for significant powers, but many unusual circumstances of their birth have created a rare situation. There is no record of a birth so blessed in all of Coventry history. Their arrival on Samhain, the most sacred night on the witch's calendar, seriously increases their potential. It had been foretold that their birth would bridge the day and night. Artemis was born listening to owls call and bats shriek, just as the full Blood Moon was setting. Two minutes later, a moment after the sun rose, Apolla was born.

A full Blood Moon on Samhain is rare indeed, occurring only once every century. Most important, the fact that they are twins means that together, they are powerful beyond imagination. Without proper education and discipline, however, and the wisdom of an ancient community to guide them, their talents can be corrupted, and their enormous gifts could also be their downfall. *Signature scents:* Artemis – lemon, patchouli, and lavender; Apolla – mint, chamomile, violets, and rosemary.

Lord Karsh Antayus, Esteemed Elder (deceased). The community mourns the recent loss of a beloved teacher and friend. As a young man, Karsh's talents were equaled only by those of his best friend, Nathaniel DuBaer. Lord Karsh tirelessly devoted himself to horticultural studies and the education of

Coventry's citizens. For the last fifteen years he was the mentor of the DuBaer twins as they grew up separately on the mainland, under the watchful care of their adoptive Protectors. *Signature scents:* cinnamon, sage, and thyme.

Che Bad

Some on Coventry Island do not live up to the creed. Caution should be exercised in dealings with any of the following individuals:

Lord Thantos DuBaer – A Master of Transmutation and a captain of industry, the eldest DuBaer brother spends much of his time on the mainland tending to his global corporation, CompUMage, and its various subsidiaries, including 3 Brothers. While the technology companies have done a lot of good both on Coventry Island and beyond, one cannot overlook Lord Thantos's less generous acts, which include shielding his fugitive nephews, kidnapping Lord Karsh, and his alleged role in the murder of his brother Aron. *Signature scents:* cloves, wet earth, and stinging ice.

Fredo DuBaer – Public Enemy #1. As Leila DuBaer herself once said, "…where did he come from, my poor Fredo? My youngest and last child. Perhaps I was too old. He was never right…" The youngest son of Nathaniel and Leila DuBaer is currently being detained on The Peninsula. He was recently convicted of the murder of his older brother Aron DuBaer, a case that went unsolved for fifteen years. *Signature scents:* poop.

Vey and Tsuris DuBaer – The sons of Fredo DuBaer are currently being sought after formal accusations of the murder of Lord Karsh failed to result in jail time for the boys. *Signature scents:* cheap cologne, hair tonic, and body odor. Note: no one can tell the brothers apart by their scents.

Sersee Tremaine – The Leader of the Furies was passed over for Initiate training by Lords Karsh, Thantos, and others, and is rumored to be lurking in the Caves of Coventry, somewhere near Luna Soleil. She is considered armed, dangerous, and profoundly arrogant. *Signature scents:* nettles and spearmint.

Sinon – A young, pimply punk, a mindless disciple of Thantos. *Signature scents:* boot leather, feet, and motor oil.

Amaryllis – Fledgling, loyal to Thantos DuBaer, who "lends her powers" so that she may do his bidding. *Signature scents:* jimson weed and nettles.

THE QUESTIONABLE

Bevin Staphylus may or may not be under the thrall of Lord Thantos DuBaer. Staphylus spends all of his time on the mainland, where he is known as "Brice Stanley." Despite Stanley's connection to Thantos, Lord Karsh saw something redeeming in his love for guardian Ileana DuBaer. *Signature scents:* magnolia, orange blossom, and Calvin Klein pour Homme.

Epee – A Fury and follower of Sersee Tremaine, Epee has never had an original thought in her life. *Signature scents:* daisies and puppy-dog tails.

Shane A. Wright was a long-time follower of Lord Thantos, and has tricked the twins, especially Apolla, many times into believing he's switched sides. He hasn't. *Signature scents:* peppermint, cedar, and clove.

Michaelina – Although this young Fury has fallen in with the evil Sersee Tremaine, Leader of the Furies, she has on occasion defied Sersee and done the right thing. *Signature scents:* hyacinth, ginseng, and clover.

MAP OF COVENTRY TODAY

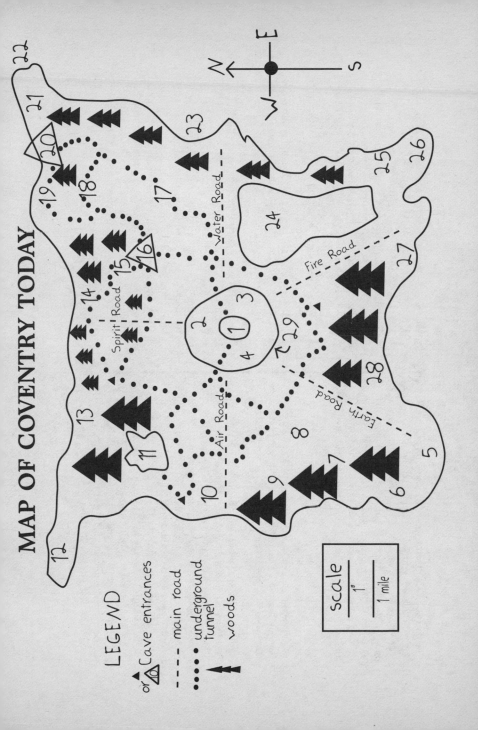

1. **The Unity Dome** – meeting place for the Unity Council; seat of Coventry courts and other civic activity

2. **The Village Plaza** – downtown Coventry, where locals shop, dine, and gather; anchored by the Food Co-op

3. **Coventry Center for Growth and Learning** – includes the Geologic Foundation, the Horticultural Society, the Airborne Arts Field, the Initiation Academy, the History Museum, the Healing Arts Society, and Coventry Clinic

4. **The Library and Archives**

5. **West Beach** – as close as curious mainlanders ever get to

6. **Antayus Cemetery** – final resting place of the Antayus clan

7. **The Swamp** – a mysterious and dangerous place; enter with caution

8. **The Cottage of Ileana DuBaer** – guardian of the DuBaer twins

9. **The Cottage of Karsh Antayus** – Tracker, Esteemed Elder, and beloved mentor of the DuBaer twins

10. **Mount Mabon** – gathering place for many public festivals

11. **Solstice Pond** – danger lurks here

12. **North Meadow** – recreation area

13. **The Peninsula** – housing the Coventry Center for Rehabilitation, set aside for dangerous witches and warlocks in need of healing and forgiveness

14. **The Impenetrable Woodlands** – Lord Karsh and Ileana DuBaer hid the newborn DuBaer twins from their uncle Thantos DuBaer in these woods.

15. **Luna Soleil** – home of Aron (deceased) and Miranda DuBaer, birthplace of Artemis and Apolla

16. **The Cave of the Furies** – the underground home of Sersee, Epie, and Michaelina (aka "The Furies")

17. **Scorpio Hill** – site of the murder of Aron DuBaer

18. **Crailmore Tunnel** – a subterranean roadway

19. **Rock Mount Cemetery** – burial grounds of the DuBaer family

20. **Crailmore Cave** – the underground mouth of the Crailmore Tunnel

21. **Crailmore** – ancestral estate of the DuBaer family

22. **The Cliffs** – the craggy landmass upon which Crailmore is built

23. **East Beach**

24. **The Abigail Vale** – nurtures the finest livestock in the world

25. **Bonfire Beach**

26. **Beltaine Hill** – gathering spot for public rituals

27. **The Faerie Wood** – a natural mainlander barrier situated behind and around the marina

28. **Harbor Haven** – site of the marina and ferry landing

29. **Eternity and Infinity Circles** – the roads that protect the Unity Dome, the Village Plaza, the Coventry Center for Growth and Learning, and the Library and Archives.

THE COVENTRY CALENDAR

THE WHEEL OF THE YEAR

YULE

SAMHAIN IMBOLG

MABON OSTARA

LUGHNASSADH BELTAINE

MIDSUMMER

Eight festivals make up the "The Wheel of the Year." The wheel symbolizes eternity, and each spoke represents a major seasonal celebration. These holidays fall on solar events, such as the first day of Spring. They divide the year with evenly spaced natural markers. There are four major and four minor festivals each year.

In addition to the eight festivals, each month has a full moon with its own special name:

MOONS	
JANUARY	WOLF MOON
FEBRUARY	ICE MOON
MARCH	STORM MOON
APRIL	GROWING MOON
MAY	HARE MOON
JUNE	MEAD MOON
JULY	HAY MOON
AUGUST	CORN MOON
SEPTEMBER	HARVEST MOON
OCTOBER	BLOOD MOON
NOVEMBER	SNOW MOON
DECEMBER	COLD MOON

Also, each day of the week is ruled by a heavenly body with special characteristics.

DAYS OF THE WEEK

SUNDAY *THE SUN*
Peace, harmony, the respect of people in high places

MONDAY *THE MOON*
Journeys, dreams, reunion, spiritual messages

TUESDAY *MARS*
Bravery, strength, undoing negative spells

WEDNESDAY *MERCURY*
Clear communications, safe travel, spiritual awareness

THURSDAY *JUPITER*
Abundance of money, health, luck

FRIDAY *VENUS*
Love, romance, beauty, happiness, friendship

SATURDAY *SATURN*
Protection, wisdom, purification

EDUCATION IN COVENTRY

In most instances, there are thirteen levels to a complete Coventry under-Initiate education. Once students are Initiated, they may wear robes of any color they like, but while at the Academy, their robes identify their level of achievement. Fledglings studying on the mainland may, of course, wear their usual clothing.

The thirteenth level is followed by a testing period, generally lasting six months to a year (although it took Fredo DuBaer three years, the longest on record). Upon demonstrating sufficient knowledge of herbs, crystals, incense, elements, incantations, ethics, and history, the new witch is fully Initiated in both a private ritual and a public ceremony held on the next full moon at the Unity Dome.

THE ACADEMY

LEVEL	NICKNAME	ROBE
FLEDGLINGS		
ONE	LIONS	PALE YELLOW
TWO	OWLS	SAFFRON
THREE	BOARS	PINK
SENSITIVES		
FOUR	NEWTS	BURNT ORANGE
FIVE	GOATS	SKY BLUE
SIX	DRAGONFLIES	BRIGHT RED
PROTECTORS		
SEVEN	EAGLES	PURPLE
EIGHT	SERPENTS	OLIVE GREEN
NINE	RAVENS	DARK CRIMSON
ADEPTS		
TEN	RAMS	LAVENDER
ELEVEN	HARES	ROYAL BLUE
TWELVE	WOLVES	BLACK
THIRTEEN	STAGS	WHITE

After Initiation, new witches and warlocks may signify their areas of excellence by bands of color sewn onto the hems or sleeves of their new robes, as follows:

ROBES		
	WHITE	PURIFICATION AND CLEANSING
	YELLOW	DIVINATION
	RED OR ORANGE	PROTECTIVE RITES
	GREEN	HERBALISM AND ECOLOGY
	BLUE	HEALING
	PURPLE	SPIRITUAL AWARENESS
	BROWN	ANIMALS
	BLACK	PROTECTION AND DIVINE ENERGY

Many choose to continue their formal education past Initiation, achieving the levels of Guardian and Tracker, which in itself includes Shapeshifter, Master of Transmutation, Mentor, and Lordship, the highest rank attainable through training alone.

Those trackers who most distinguish themselves with long service to Coventry Island and the education and protection of healers everywhere may some day be named "Esteemed Elders" during a vote held annually by the Unity Council.

MAGICK ITEMS

Herbs, oils, crystals, and all the rest can be used in varying amounts and combinations, some as yet unknown, and with as many different incantations as there are practitioners. (Extensive information about tools is available at Coventry Island's many libraries, museums, and schools).

TOOLS		
	BOOK OF SHADOWS	*MORTAR AND PESTLE, RUNES*
	BESOM (BROOM)	*OIL, SALT*
	CAULDRON	*PENDULUM, SEEDS*
	CRYSTALS AND GEMS	*PENTACLE, STRING*
	HERBS	*ROBE, WANDS*

ⱨERBS

Different herbs apply to different types of magick. See page 29 for a chart.

It is always best when one's own land and labor produce the tools used in healing, but that isn't always possible. Coventry Island is blessed with abundant copper, iron, fluorite, and gypsum, and grows dozens of varieties of useful flowers, trees,

HERBS

PURPOSE	HERB
Beauty	Orange Blossom
Clairvoyance	Lavender
Comfort	Cypress
Courage	Cedar
Ease Feelings of Loss	Cypress
Energy	Peppermint
Fidelity	Clover, Nutmeg
Friendship	Passion Flower
Hair Growth	Magnolia
Happiness	Lavender
Harmony	Bayberry, Lily of the Valley, Narcissus
Healing	Allspice, Cedar, Cinnamon, Eucalyptus, Gardenia, Jasmine, Pine
Health	Ginseng, Jasmine, Mistletoe, Nutmeg
Hex-Breaking	Cedar
Honesty	Honeysuckle
Love	Cherry, Cinnamon, Clove, Clover, Gardenia, Ginger, Plumeria, Peppermint, Orange, Lavender, Jasmine, Hibiscus, Hyacinth, Lily of the Valley, Mistletoe, Orange Blossom
Luck	Allspice, Bayberry, Ginseng, Nutmeg, Orange
Memory	Honeysuckle
Money	Allspice, Almond, Bayberry, Cedar, Clove, Pine, Patchouli, Nutmeg, Jasmine, Ginger, Honeysuckle, Orange
Peace	Amber, Bayberry, Gardenia, Lavender, Lily of the Valley, Magnolia, Narcissus, Passion Flower
Power	Cinnamon, Ginger
Prosperity	Almond
Protection	Cedar, Cinnamon, Clove, Clover, Eucalyptus, Frankincense, Hyacinth, Lavender, Mistletoe, Patchouli, Pine
Self-Confidence	Amber
Sleep	Jasmine, Lavender, Passion Flower
Spirituality	Frankincense, Gardenia
Stability	Amber
Success	Cinnamon, Clover, Ginger
Wisdom	Almond

and herbs. But many essential items—tiger's eye, for example—originate in places as far away as Africa, and must be imported and purchased for use.

STONES AND CRYSTALS

Like herbs, different stones and/or crystals can help a witch achieve a variety of goals and desires.

PURPOSE	STONES
Astral Projection	Quartz Crystals, Opal
Beauty	Amber, Tiger's Eye, Opal, Jasper
Money, Wealth, and Business	Bloodstone, Citrine, Malachite, Green Tourmaline
Courage	Agate, Amethyst, Bloodstone, Lapis, Turquoise
Defensive Magick	Mica, Onyx, Sapphire, Black Tourmaline
Divination	Azurite, Hematite, Mica, Moonstone, Obsidian
Dreams	Amethyst, Azurite
Friendship	Rose Quartz, Pink Tourmaline, Turquoise
Happiness	Amethyst, Sunstone
Healing and Health	Amber, Amethyst, Aventurine, Bloodstone, Hematite, Sunstone, Turquoise
Luck	Amber, Apache Tear, Opal, Tiger's Eye, Turquoise
Peace	Calcite, Coral, Malachite, Blue Tourmaline
Physical Strength	Agate, Amber, Bloodstone, Diamond, Garnet
Protection	Amber, Apache Tear, Calcite, Citrine
Travel	Moonstone
Sleep	Moonstone, Peridot, Blue Tourmaline
Wisdom	Coral, Jade, Sodalite

STONES CRYSTALS

ESSENTIAL OILS

PURPOSE	ESSENCE
Courage	Cedar, Musk, Rose Geranium
Friendship	Stephanotis, Sweetpea
Happiness	Apple Blossom, Sweetpea, Tuberose
Harmony	Basil, Gardenia, Lilac, Narcissus
Healing	Carnation, Eucalyptus, Gardenia, Lotus, Myrrh, Narcissus, Rosemary, Sandalwood, Violet
Hex-Breaking	Bergamont, Myrrh, Rose Geranium, Rosemary, Rue, Vertivert
Love	Clove, Gardenia, Jasmine, Orris, Plumeria,
Luck	Rose, Sweetpea, Cinnamon, Cypress, Lotus
Magnetism (attract men)	Ambergris, Gardenia, Ginger, Jasmine, Lavender, Musk, Neroli, Tonka
Magnetism (attract women)	Bay, Civet, Musk, Patchouli, Stephanotis, Vertivert, Violet
Mental Prowess	Honeysuckle, Lilac, Rosemary
Money	Almond, Bayberry, Bergamot, Honeysuckle, Mint, Patchouli, Pine, Vervain
Peace	Benzoin, Cumin, Gardenia, Hyacinth, Magnolia, Rose, Tuberose
Power	Carnation, Rosemary, Vanilla
Protection	Cypress, Myrrh, Patchouli, Rose Geranium, Rosemary, Rue, Violet, Wisteria
Psychic Powers	Acacia, Anise, Cassia, Heliotrope, Lemongrass, Lilac, Mimosa, Nutmeg, Sandalwood, Purification Acacia, Cinnamon, Clove, Frankincense, Jasmine, Lavender
Sleep	Lavender, Narcissus
Spirituality	Heliotrope, Lotus, Magnolia, Sandalwood
Vitality	Allspice, Carnation, Rosemary Vanilla

THE COVENTRY CREED

Coventry citizens have a deep connection with Nature's laws. We embrace and nurture all creatures, great and small.

A true witch seeks to control the forces within herself or himself in order to live wisely and well, in unity with all, and harming no other. There are those who may, out of ignorance or intention, misuse their precious skills. They are held to account at tribunals presided over by Coventry's Esteemed Elders at the Unity Dome.

Witchcraft is not a cult. We do not try to get others to follow us as their leaders. We do, however, welcome to our community all who show their goodness and gifts, and choose to call themselves witches. We do not interfere with the free will of others in the practice of our own magick. In short, "Harm None" is the whole of the law.

IT IS EXPECTED THAT ONE WILL

Hold all life in respect and reverence;
practice healing with humility, education, discipline, and
the wisdom of the ancient community;
handle all beings with maturity, honor, and good sense;
take all one is given, and give all of oneself.

IT IS FORBIDDEN TO

Seek power through the suffering of any living thing;
enchant or otherwise meddle in the lives of others
except for their good, not one's own;
put one's own desires above what is necessary.

We live by upholding the wisdom that is
inscribed on the Unity dome:

"THAT ALL THINGS MIGHT GROW TO THEIR MOST BOUNTIFUL GOODNESS."

LOOK FOR
T⊙WITCHES #10
DESTINY'S TWINS

It's the moment they've been waiting for. Cam and Alex are about to be initiated. But first, the girls must complete a series of tricky tests and challenges. Only then will they be welcomed as true witches in a blowout bash on Coventry.

But *someone* doesn't want Cam and Alex to succeed. And that someone will do whatever it takes to stop the twins from achieving their destiny.

AVAILABLE FEBRUARY 2004 WHEREVER BOOKS ARE SOLD!